The
BOY *with the*
BUTTERFLY
MIND

Praise for
Victoria Williamson

The Boy with the Butterfly Mind

'What a masterclass in empathy. This book gave me such
a terrific insight into how ADHD affects a young boy and
those around him. It is a great reminder that we shouldn't
automatically judge others. I was rooting for Jamie and Elin!'

Lisa Thompson, author of *The Goldfish Boy*

'Moving. Powerful. Relevant. Contemporary storytelling at
its very best. Another triumph from Victoria Williamson,
tackling important issues relevant to kids
in a powerful and moving way.'

Juliette Forrest, author of *Twister*

'My heart broke and soared by turns in this inspiring story of two
kids who seem to have nothing in common but a desperate desire
for their family to be whole.'

Shari Green, author of ALA Schneider Award winner
Macy McMillan and the Rainbow Goddess

'Truly sensational. Told through two voices and suffused with
real heart; empathy and emotionally-invested storytelling
at its best that has so much to teach today's children.
My heart genuinely aches. A must, must, must read.'

Scott Evans, The Reader Teacher

'Full of hope, empathy and true acceptance. I love how the characters' points of view are honest.'

Marla Conn, Read-ability

'Fantastic to have a book about ADHD and by such a sensitive writer. So helpful for empathy, understanding and identity. Everyone needs to see themselves in books.'

Chloe Daykin, author of *Fish Boy*

The Fox Girl and the White Gazelle

'Williamson movingly makes it clear that working-class solidarity traverses borders, race, ethnicity, and religion.'

Kirkus Reviews, Starred Review

'Delightfully nuanced, diverse [and] thoughtful.'

Youth Services Book Review, Starred Review

'An essential read in today's political climate.'

Lu Hersey, *Mslexia* Children's Book Award-winning author of *Deep Water*

'Relevant, moving, and quite extraordinary.'

Lucy Coats, author of the *Beasts of Olympus* series

'A touching, thought-provoking adventure.'

The Bookseller

'Beautifully written, touching, and inspiring.'

Nikki Sheehan, twice Carnegie-nominated author of *Swan Boy* and *Goodnight, Boy*

Also by Victoria Williamson

The Fox Girl and the White Gazelle

For Granny and Grandad, who helped weave many of
the golden stories of my childhood, which I spin into
the threads of my novels today.

Kelpies is an imprint of Floris Books
First published in 2019 by Floris Books
© 2019 Victoria Williamson

The publisher acknowledges subsidy from Creative Scotland
towards the publication of this volume.

 Also available as an eBook

British Library CIP Data available
ISBN 978-178250-600-3
Printed in Poland through Hussar

 Floris Books supports sustainable forest management
by printing this book on materials made from wood that
comes from responsible sources and reclaimed material

The
BOY *with* *the*
BUTTERFLY
MIND

VICTORIA WILLIAMSON

Kelpies

Part One

Hanging On

Elin

The summer holidays felt like they'd ended a hundred years ago. We'd only been back at school a few weeks, but already everyone hated the Friday morning maths test.

Not me. I studied way too hard to get nervous answering a few easy sums, even if Miss Morrison was a dragon who handed out extra work to anyone who even sneezed too loud. I had nothing to worry about. I'd never been in trouble for anything in my whole life.

"Write out twenty-four million, sixty-two thousand and seventeen in numbers," she roared, shattering the silence into twenty-four million, sixty-two thousand and seventeen little pieces. I could almost see the fire from the Dragon's breath singeing Lauren's hair as she stopped trying to copy my work and stared blankly at her own book, the numbers already forgotten.

Ha! Jellybean brain. That's what you get for cheating and not paying attention.

I bit back a grin at how easy the question was, and wrote the answer neatly below the last one, making sure to use my best handwriting. The girl sitting beside me shuffled closer, and I could hear her sniffing noises getting louder. Paige Munro's runny nose was like a warning siren. A couple more questions she couldn't answer and she'd be crying all over her maths jotter. My hand flew across my book to cover my answers, and I leaned forward, protecting my work from the hungry eyes of the other kids who were either too stupid to do a few easy sums, or too lazy to study. Why should I share anything with them? They all hated me no matter what I did.

"Can I see just this one?" Paige whispered. Her voice was quivering like her bottom lip was about to fall off. I glanced over at her. Behind her big glasses, her eyes were filling with nervous tears and her nose was streaming with the effort to hold them back. She was so scared of Miss Morrison it was pathetic. I edged further away in my seat. I could smell the pickled onion crisps she'd had for breakfast, and her stringy brown hair was almost as greasy as her fingers. No wonder I'd nicknamed her 'the Slug' in my head. Didn't she ever wash?

"Please, Elin? If I get bad marks again Miss Morrison will be furious."

"Not my problem," I hissed under my breath, shifting my gaze back to my own maths book so the Dragon wouldn't catch me talking.

Miss Morrison shuffled the paper on her desk, ready to read out the next question, and the whole class held their breath again.

By the time the test was done, my book was filled with a whole row of neat answers, and the other kids were glaring at me like they wanted me to drop dead. I avoided their eyes as we handed in our work and took out our creative writing jotters. I could almost hear the class sighing with relief now that the test was over and we could work on our stories instead. We were doing a history project about the Vikings, and my story was about a Scottish girl from my home town who got kidnapped and taken away on their ship. Luckily I'd already finished it, because there was no way I could concentrate on Viking raids and longboats right now. Everyone else had relaxed, but I was chewing my lip so hard it hurt. I kept glancing up at Miss Morrison, watching her frowning and tutting over her marking, and praying that the big red crosses she was drawing with her pen weren't being made in my book.

You have to get everything right! the little voice at the back of my head whispered to me. *You have to be perfect! It's the only way to win your dad back!*

I KNOW! I whispered back. *I'm doing my best!*

I must've said that last bit out loud, as Rachel nudged Lauren, pointing at me and sniggering. Rachel was a mean troll who'd been picking on me for years. I wasn't going to give her the satisfaction of letting her see she was getting to me. I sat up straighter to show I didn't care, slipped a sheet of paper from the back of my project folder, and started writing the next chapter of the only story that mattered to me.

The Princess was trapped in the Dungeon, watched over by the fiery Dragon. The hideous Troll sat in a corner of the dark cell sharpening its poisoned arrows, ready to attack. A foul stench of pickled onion filled the whole room, and the Princess whirled round to see the hungry Slug slithering over the floor towards her. One touch of its slimy skin would be enough to kill her. The Princess had to escape fast, or she'd lose her chance to rescue the King forever.

Suddenly there was a loud clattering of hooves on the bars blocking the window. Her faithful horse Athena had come to her rescue!

"Good girl, Athena!" the Princess called, dodging out of the way as one of the Troll's poisoned arrows whizzed past her ear. "Just one more kick and I'll be free!"

The hooves clattered down again, and the bars gave way with a crash. The Princess leapt up and grabbed hold of her horse's silky mane just in time to avoid the Slug's deadly slime. Together they rode off to rescue the King from the Tower, where he was being kept prisoner by the Wicked Witch and her —

"Elin, did you hear me?"

Miss Morrison was looking straight at me, and my heart skipped a beat before her frown changed into a smile.

"Very good work," she nodded approvingly, holding up my maths book so that everyone could see the gold star she'd stuck to the page. "Perfect marks as always."

I let out a long breath and smiled back. But the smile didn't last long, and neither did the warm glow from Miss Morrison's praise. Ever since Dad left it seemed like there was a hole inside me, where all the good feelings got lost. It was cold and dark in there, like he took a piece of me with him when he went away. Maybe if I held on tightly to the fairy tale in my head, collected enough gold stars and was as perfect as the princess in my story, I might just have a chance to win Dad back.

I sharpened my pencil, turned the paper over, and set to work. This had to be the best story ever.

2

Jamie

"Did you get that last word, Jamie?" The way Mr Patel says it I can tell he's had to repeat the question. I nod, even though I have no idea what the last word in the spelling test was. I lost it somewhere between listening to Ryan blowing his runny nose like he's trying to play the tuba, and watching Claire nervously ripping her notebook into confetti. Mr Patel says I distract the other kids, but it's really the other way round.

I sit up straighter, ready to catch the next word when it comes my way, but this time it's the weather that has it in for me.

Bullets of rain are hitting the windows so hard I swear it's like trying to take a test in the middle of a war zone. Which is kind of funny, since we're doing a project on World War Two this year, and I've been looking up loads of stuff on the internet about different kinds of weapons. The planes were so cool – the Mosquitoes were superfast, and the Spitfires were made right here in Southampton! How awesome is that? Germany had these amazing tanks called Panzers, but the Tiger tanks were better, they could—

"ACCOMMODATE," Mr Patel says again. "Ac-commo-date. Jamie, are you writing this down?"

I snatch up my pen from the floor where it's rolled and try to find a free space on my test sheet to write the word. My handwriting's a bit of a mess, and it's not easy trying to squeeze the big words onto such a little line. Maybe that's part of the test too. Maybe that's why I always fail.

Ak, I write, then I cross it out and try *A-c-k-o*… No, that's not right either. I scribble over it too hard and accidentally knock over the stack of books and pen holders I've built into a mini castle all round my desk. They go cascading onto the floor like a waterfall, and I leap after them like one of those Olympic divers jumping off the high board. I'm so busy gathering books and pens up I barely hear the laughter of the other kids. I'm used to it. It washes over me now in waves and I just drift along with it.

"Jamie, will you PLEASE sit down!" Mr Patel sounds like he's running out of patience. It's the second year in a row that I'm in his class, and I don't think he can take another three terms of me and my craziness.

"Emigrate!" he snaps, snatching my test sheet from under my desk and slapping it down in front of me. "Write. It. Down."

"I AM writing it," I mutter, fishing around in my wrecked castle walls for a pen and crossing out my last attempt in a big red scribble. Oh, damn. Wrong pen. It looks like my nose has bled all over my spelling sheet now. I had a nosebleed once. It was so bad Mum had to take me to A & E cos it wouldn't stop, and the nurse said it was the worst case she'd seen in—

"EMIGRATE!" Mr Patel is bellowing at me now, and the other kids have stopped smiling and are starting to look annoyed. I'm holding things up. The sooner we get this test done the sooner we can go back to making our World War Two tank models. Mine's a Tiger. I was going to do a Panzer, but—

NO! Emigrate. Write the word down, you fruit loop.

I hold my pen tight and write *E-m-y*, then I change the *y* to an *i*. Then I try to fit in another *m*. Then I run out of space. I sigh and hunt for my black pen to try to write over the mess. This test would be a whole lot easier if I'd remembered to study for it. I'm not good at remembering things. I'm not much good at anything except causing trouble.

"Regulate," Mr Patel says, rolling the 'r' like it's stuck to his teeth and his tongue's tripping over it.

Wait! What was that last word? It was important.

I go spelunking down into the big hole in my head where all my thoughts get swallowed up, and come back up holding tight to the word I don't want to forget.

Emigrate. That was it.

That's what Mum and me are going to do very soon. Emigrate to America with her boyfriend Chris, and leave all the bad memories behind. It'll be a fresh start there, a new life. Maybe I'll forget all the nights I lay in bed when I was younger listening to Mum and Dad yelling at each other down in the kitchen about my behaviour. Maybe I'll forget the times the rage took over and made me scream at the top of my voice in frustration. Maybe I'll be able to have an operation to fix my brain so I can concentrate and think like normal people.

Maybe in America they can find a way to cure my craziness.

"And the final word – ALTERNATE," Mr Patel calls, scowling at me to make sure I heard it. I smile back at him. It's exactly the word I was thinking of. I'd almost given up hope of being anything but the boy who can't concentrate for more than half a second before his mind's fluttering off somewhere else like a butterfly, but now I'm getting a chance to give my story an *alternate* ending.

This time I'm going to make sure it's a happy one.

Elin

"You think you're really clever, don't you?"

Rachel was standing over me, blocking the sunlight with her big mean face. Her hands were on her hips and her eyes were all screwed up and angry. I knew why the Troll was mad. She'd got bad marks again. I didn't see how her being stupid was my fault though.

But I didn't say that out loud. I just gulped and shrugged and stared at my library book, hoping she'd go away.

"Why are you always such a stuck-up swot?" Rachel snapped, trying to get my attention.

"Yeah," Lauren chimed in, "why are you such a swot, Elin?"

Out of the corner of my eye I could see another group of kids stop their game of dodgeball and edge closer to my bench, eager to see if we were going to fight. They should have known by now they were wasting their time. I wasn't brave like the Perfect Princess in my story. I wouldn't fight back even if the Troll punched me in the face.

"Everyone hates you, Elin. Except Miss Morrison. You're her special pet," Rachel scowled.

"Yeah," Lauren echoed, "you and the teacher should get married and spend all your time doing maths together."

The other kids all laughed. I swallowed hard and tried to concentrate on the words on the page. I could barely see them through the tears blurring my eyes, and my hands were starting to shake so badly I almost dropped my book. I kept my head down and propped my book up in my lap so it looked like I was just ignoring them. That made Rachel even madder, and she snatched it off me and flung it across the playground.

"You want to be Miss Morrison's pet? There. Go and fetch."

"Yeah, go and fetch it, Elin."

Leave me alone or I'll chop you to bits with my sword! the Perfect Princess yelled at them inside my head, but I wasn't brave enough to say it out loud. My fingers curled round the sharp pencil in my pocket, clutching it tightly for protection as the laughter got louder. I could feel my cheeks burning, my throat aching with the effort not to cry. Perfect Princesses never cried, I knew that for sure. It was the last thing Dad told me before he moved out.

I could still remember the sad look on Dad's face as he crouched down on the doorstep to hug me the night he left.

"I need you to be brave, Elin, and not cry, can you do that for me?"

"Yes Dad," I'd whispered, my throat so tight I could barely get the words out. *"I'll be good, I promise!"*

"That's my perfect little princess."

But I wasn't perfect. If I was then Dad would never have left. It was my fault he was gone.

"Are we playing dodgeball or what?" Steven was getting bored and wanted to go back to the game.

I never gave them the satisfaction of seeing me cry or losing my temper, and watching Rachel and Lauren throw insults at me wasn't as much fun as the other kids had hoped.

"Fine. Let's play. Little Miss Boring Swot's not worth it anyway."

They all walked away to finish their game, but not before Rachel kicked the ball at me so hard it stung as it slapped off my leg. Darren scooped it up and ran off with it, and I was left staring in horror at the big muddy patch on my white socks.

I snatched a packet of tissues from my pocket, feeling sick at the sight of the brown stain smeared across the pretty lace edging. I *hated* being dirty. Dad worked in a lab when I was little, and used to joke that he was a clean freak because he knew exactly how many germs were growing in the dishes when they were left by the sink, or in the dirty clothes overflowing from the laundry basket. Then he stopped laughing about it, and he and Mum started rowing about it instead. If only I'd done more to help. If only I'd cleaned the dishes instead of having dolls' tea parties, or put the laundry in the machine instead of watching cartoons, or—

A big fat tear was threatening to escape from the corner of my eye. I brushed it away angrily and pulled my pencil from my pocket. Checking to make sure no one was watching, I started scribbling frantically on a piece of paper I'd taken from my project folder.

"Bring her to me so I can bottle her tears!" the Troll roared. "I will cast a spell so the King will forget he ever had a daughter – just one tear will be enough to seal her fate!"

"One tear!" the Troll's shadow echoed. "Make her cry just one tear!"

Suddenly a goblin's arrow caught Athena across one snow-white leg and she stumbled, sending the Princess tumbling into the marsh. Her feet began to sink into the magical mud as the goblin army closed in.

"Bring her tears to me!" the Troll cackled.

"Yes, bring her tears!" the Shadow echoed.

"You'll never make me cry, never!" The brave Princess drew her diamond sword, and the goblins fell back, howling in fear. She raised the weapon above the cowering Troll's head and —

"Is this yours?" a shy voice asked. My library book was placed back in my lap so suddenly I jumped, and the point of my pencil broke.

I looked up. Paige Munro was smiling at me hopefully through her thick glasses.

"Of course it's mine!" I snapped, annoyed by the interruption. The Slug had just seen the Troll fling my book halfway across the playground, so who else did she think it belonged to?

I shoved my notepad in my pocket again and went back to cleaning my sock, but ignoring people didn't seem to be working so well for me today. Paige kept trying, sitting down beside me and asking, "Is it a good book? What's it about?"

Before I could stop her, she'd taken the book from me again, thumbing through it with her greasy fingers. Just as well it was a library book, or I'd have to disinfect it before putting it back on my bookshelf at home.

"Oh! There's a princess in it. I like princess stories. Can I borrow it?"

"Fine." I rolled my eyes. "Give it back to me at home time though, and don't lick your fingers when you turn the pages or anything manky like that, OK?" Anything to get her to leave me alone.

I left her sitting there and walked away towards the group of playground supervisors who were chatting by the bins, putting as much distance as I could between me and Paige. I didn't want anyone thinking we were friends. Paige's clothes weren't washed more than once a week, and she never had enough money for snacks or school trips. She was the only person in the class more unpopular than me, and if I started hanging around with her then I might get picked last in PE instead.

I wasn't desperate enough for friends to be seen dead talking to the Slug.

"Look at the state of this place," one of the playground supervisors was saying. "You'd think they'd held a music festival here at the weekend."

Despite the sunshine, September had blown in like a tornado, and empty juice bottles and crisp packets from the overturned bins were strewn all around the playground. I couldn't do anything about my dirty sock until I got home, but this was one mess that the Perfect Princess could sort out. I rolled up my sleeves and got to work, borrowing a litter picker from one of the supervisors to collect bottles and wrappers and put them back in the bins. By the time the bell rang I'd cleared half the playground, and the supervisors were smiling and saying nice things about me that I pretended not to hear.

"Well done Elin, you're such a good girl."

"We could do with a few more like you at this school."

I grinned secretly to myself, but the happy feeling faded as soon as I lined up with the rest of my class to go back inside. I could hear them whispering about me, and even though I tried to shut their mean words out, Lauren's voice was just too loud.

"Yeah. She's always sucking up to the teachers. No wonder she doesn't have any friends."

She was right. I didn't have any friends.

It was lonely being so perfect all the time.

4

Jamie

"Why do you always have to be so STUPID all the time?"

"It's not my fault!" I yell back. "You're changing the rules! It's always a throw-in when the ball goes over the line. You can't just make it a free kick whenever you want!"

There's a loud buzzing noise building up inside my head, and my fists are clenching and unclenching in frustration. Why won't they just *listen* to me?

"How are we meant to have a throw-in, genius?" Ryan sniffs, blowing his nose again. Him and his runny nose are driving me insane. "There's a puddle the size of the Atlantic over there."

If I could take a deep breath and step back for one second, I'd see that he was right. But of course I can't do that. I can't do anything except fight the waves of anger that are crashing over me.

"You can't just change the rules!" I yell again. I'm close to tears. I hate it when they change things halfway through a game. I get all confused and it's hard for me to concentrate on what I'm meant to be doing.

"Look, does anyone else apart from Freak-Boy have a problem with it being a free kick instead of a throw-in?" Ryan asks.

"Nah," Luke says, "let's just get on with it."

The storm in my head is threatening to burst, and I can feel my face going bright red as all the blood rushes up to my hyperactive brain. I'm breathing so hard I feel faint, but I stand my ground. It's like I'm stuck in a robot body that's out of control, and I can't find the off button.

"Jamie man, calm down, huh? It's just a game." Luke makes the mistake of putting his hand on my shoulder, and all hell breaks loose.

I HATE being touched. It's like someone scratching their nails down a blackboard while force-feeding me lemons and farting in my face as they walk over my grave.

"GET YOUR HANDS OFF ME!"

"Hey! What's your problem? Just—"

"THERE'S YOUR FREE KICK!"

My body's in motion, and before I can find the brakes, my foot lashes out so hard at the ball that it goes flying ten feet into the air and sails clean over the wire link fence surrounding the football pitch. There's total silence for a long moment as everyone stands and watches the ball bounce across the main road, then there's a horrible shrieking of car brakes and blaring of horns as it weaves in and out of the traffic. The other kids all turn on me.

"What the hell, Jamie?"

"You crazy FREAK!"

"How are we meant to finish our game now, you psycho?"

"I DON'T CARE!"

24

Before my overheated brain can cool down, my legs have already taken over again and I'm running across the pitch, splashing straight through puddles and racing round the side of the school. I don't slow down till I'm well out of sight of the senior playground. We're not meant to be anywhere near the staff car park, but it's the only quiet place on the school grounds. Sometimes I just need to get away from everyone else. If they would just back off and let me THINK then maybe I'd be able to control my temper.

The rage drains as quickly as it appeared, leaving a big empty hole in the pit of my stomach. I feel cold and shivery, but I'm not going to waste any time thinking about the angry shouts of the other kids or the ball bouncing away across the road. My butterfly mind's already moved on.

I take a deep breath and bend down to tuck in the shoelace that nearly sent me falling on my face. Mum's tried to get me to tie them more times than she can count, but I always forget, and anyway it's quicker just tucking them under my socks.

There's a big stone next to my scuffed shoes, and I pick it up, throwing it up in the air and catching it a few times. It would be cool if I had one of those catapults that can send stones halfway into space, or near enough. Maybe if I ask Dad he might get me one for Christmas. He usually gets me what I want. I think he feels guilty for moving away to Scotland when he and Mum divorced, but he shouldn't. It wasn't his fault everything got so bad. It was mine.

I could ask Mum's boyfriend Chris for a catapult, but I don't think he'd buy me one. I don't think he likes me much. Maybe I can get a catapult when we move to America in a few weeks.

I wonder if Mum's told the school I'm leaving yet? I don't think she's got my passport sorted, and I need a visa to go to the States, so she'd better hurry up.

I chuck the stone away, and it bounces off the lamppost by the row of teachers' cars with a loud zinging noise. I pick up another stone, hitting the lamppost further up and making a slightly different sound. Huh. That's cool. I wonder if I can get a job as a concert lamppost player?

I pick up a whole handful of stones and chuck them one by one at the metal post, trying to play a tune. Maybe if I added a drumbeat and bass I could make a dance track, or with a bit of hammering I could make the lamppost into one of those Caribbean steel drums.

Hey! I wonder if I can play more than one note at the same time?

I pick up another handful of stones and chuck the whole lot at the lamppost as hard as I can. Some of them bounce off the metal, but some of them don't. There's a slow-motion moment as I watch the stones that miss it fly on towards the row of cars behind, and a sick feeling in the pit of my stomach builds as I realise what's going to happen.

Why-oh-why do I never see these things coming?

I close my eyes. I don't want to watch.

There's a loud rattling of stones off a car door, and a smashing of glass. When I finally open my eyes I see big dents in the door of the red car at the end of the row, and long spiderweb cracks in both side windows. My mouth is dry with dread and my brain's whirring round and round, but it's not sending any instructions to my feet to get them to move.

Do something! Get out of here before someone sees you!

I try to override my brain's controls, but the pilot's not listening and I'm frozen in horror, staring at the wreck and waiting for all hell to break loose.

It doesn't take long. The car park's right across from the staffroom, and the teachers are all staring out of the windows. Mr Patel and the head teacher are already marching towards me.

"Jamie Lee!" the head teacher bellows. "Come here right now!"

Uh-oh. My feet are itching. I know that feeling well, and I try to ignore it, but it won't go away. It just keeps building and building till it feels like my legs are burning.

"Why do you never stop and THINK before you do something stupid?" Mr Patel yells when he gets close enough to see the mess I've made of his car.

Now is not the time to run away. Now's the time to stand and face what I've done. But before I can tell that to my feet, they're off again and I'm running back through the playground, ignoring the ringing bell and the jeers of the other kids who can tell I've got myself into trouble again. We're not allowed out of the school gates during class hours, so of course the gates are exactly where I'm headed.

I have to get away from everyone. I have to be on my own so I can try to make sense of all the white noise fogging up my head and making it hard to think straight. I have to hide away from the whole world so I can try to keep out of trouble for just five minutes.

It's lonely being so bad all the time.

Elin

"Hi Elin, did you have a good day at school?"

Mum's boyfriend Paul was in the kitchen making Chinese dumplings for dinner when I got home. I took off my shoes and put them on the rack in the cupboard by the door, hanging my jacket up neatly on a hook and putting my dirty sock straight in the laundry basket.

"It was great," I lied. "I got full marks in my maths test." That wasn't a lie, at least.

I was pretty sure one lie and one truth cancelled each other out, just like a positive and a negative sign. That was the maths of sweet-talking adults, and I was every bit as good at that as I was at arithmetic.

"That's brilliant, pet." Paul gave me a big smile as he filled the small circles of dough with stuffing and began pinching the ends together to form dumplings. "How about we have ice cream for dessert and watch a film tonight to celebrate?"

I smiled back weakly, making sure I wasn't too friendly. He wasn't my dad, he was just an imposter. I definitely didn't want him getting too comfy here. It would make it even harder to get rid of him when I managed to find a way to get my real dad back.

"If Mum's not too tired," I shrugged, so he'd know I wasn't really interested. "Aren't you working tonight?"

"I'm not due in until nine. There's plenty of time to have some family fun."

This isn't your family! I felt like yelling at him so he'd finally get it through his thick, grinning head. He'd been extra-specially nice to me for the last few days, and I was starting to get suspicious about what he and Mum were cooking up together.

I bit my tongue and picked up a sponge instead, filling the basin to do the dishes. Paul was a nurse at the local hospital, and despite his changing shifts he always managed to make sure he was home for me getting back from school, which really annoyed me. I'd rather have the house to myself while I waited for Mum to get back from her office.

"Oh, don't worry about that!" Paul took the sponge off me. "You go and watch TV or play with your friends. Dinner will be ready for your mum coming back at six, OK?"

Watch TV or play with my friends?

Wow. Paul really didn't know me at all.

I heaved a sigh like he was making my whole life a huge effort and carried my schoolbag to my room, closing the door firmly to shut out his cheerful humming. Paul had been living with us for over a year now, and he still hadn't got his head round the fact that I didn't like computer games, preferred reading to watching TV, and had no friends who weren't imaginary.

Dad understood me, I thought sadly. *He'd take me to the library if he was here tonight instead of force-feeding me sugar and making me watch rubbish films.*

Except my dad wasn't here in Bishopbriggs, or anywhere near Glasgow. He was in Edinburgh with his fake family. There'd be no trip to the library with him, and no curling up on the sofa to read to each other.

Don't think about that! I told myself, taking out my paint box and a little plaster of Paris butterfly that I hadn't finished decorating. It didn't help distract me though. It just reminded me of the summer gala we went to before Dad left. He'd sat up late with me the night before, helping me paint a giant pair of butterfly wings in beautiful colours. I'd won first prize for the best costume at that fair, and the whole afternoon I felt like I could fly. Three days later Dad packed his bags and left, and I felt like he'd taken my wings and the blue summer sky with him. Without him I wasn't a butterfly any more. I was just a caterpillar, holding on to a leaf as tight as I could and trying not to fall.

The colours on the plaster butterfly smudged, and I realised my hands were shaking so badly I couldn't hold the paintbrush straight. I put it down, looking round my spotless room for something I could tidy to help me calm down. Every surface was filled with the pottery figures I'd painted since Dad left. There were fairies and elves on my bookshelf, mermaids and unicorns on my dressing table, turreted castles on the shelf along one wall, and a whole collection of kings and queens and armoured knights on my desk. I needed all the inspiration I could get to keep holding on to my fairy-tale future.

I might not have any real friends, but at least I had a pretend one at home. I picked up the little pottery horse that was sitting on my bedside table, smiling as the crystals I'd glued across her back sparkled in the light.

"You're always right here when I need you, aren't you, Athena?" I whispered.

Dad had bought the pottery horse for my birthday two years ago, and she was the most precious thing I owned. I'd spent hours painting her eyes with a tiny brush so they looked real, and curving the corner of her mouth just right so it seemed like she was smiling back at me.

"One day when Dad comes back and Mum's not struggling for money any more, we'll move back home and I'll get to ride a horse like you for real," I told her. Mum had said I could start the riding lessons I'd always dreamed of when I turned ten, but the divorce spoiled everything. I'd be twelve in a few months, and money was so tight I'd be lucky just to get the birthday party I'd been planning in my head all year, never mind any decent presents.

I put Athena down and gazed at the photos pinned round my bed. There was one of me with Lindsay and Olivia from my old school, back when I'd actually had friends. The rest were all of me and Mum and Dad at our old house in Whitburn. That was the life I wanted, not this pretend one where Paul the Imposter was here instead of Dad, and we lived in a rubbish house miles away from my real home.

I could feel the anger starting to bubble up inside me again, and I swallowed it down quickly, afraid of what would happen if I let it out. The pain in my chest was hard to ignore, so I sat down at my desk and started up my computer, trying to distract myself with homework. But before I could open my project folder, I saw a new message waiting for me in my email inbox.

It was from Dad.

I dropped my homework book and clicked on it eagerly. When he first moved out three years ago he used to call me every night. Then after a while it was every weekend. Ever since the Wicked Witch's mutant baby came along I'd been lucky to get an email once a week. I tried not to think about what that meant for my chances of getting him to come home.

Dad *had* to come back. There was no other way my story could end.

I leaned forward and gobbled up the words on the screen.

Hi Princess,

Sorry I haven't written in a while. Sue's work's been manic, and your wee sister's had a bout of chickenpox that's kept me up every night for a week. Beth's two-and-a-half now, and looks just like you did at her age. I've attached a couple of pictures of our camping trip last month. Sorry you didn't want to come with us, I know these changes have been tough for you. Maybe when Sue gets a day off she can look after Beth and I can drive over to Glasgow and take you out for the day. I'm sorry I had to cancel the last few times when I couldn't get a childminder for Beth. This time I won't let you down, pet.

I've got to go, your wee sister's just woken up from her nap.

See you at your Gran's next week ☺

Lots of love from me and Sue and Beth,

Dad x

I let out the breath I hadn't realised I'd been holding, and saved his picture files without opening them. Later I'd crop all the photos so only Dad was in them, before adding them to my special family album. His fake wife Sue and her little brat didn't belong in there.

But it wasn't just the photos that needed to be fixed. The story Dad was telling me was all wrong too. I grabbed a pen and a sheet of paper, and started writing a better story.

The King was lonely in the Tower where he'd been trapped by the Wicked Witch. All day long he was locked inside with her mutant child, scrubbing the floors of his prison and washing her foul-smelling clothes, while she gathered herbs in the forest for her evil spells. The Mutant was always hungry and sick, and never gave the King a moment's rest.

The Wicked Witch guarded the King jealously, trying to make him forget his real home and family. But one day when she was out and the Mutant was asleep, he tiptoed to the window and whistled for a raven to come and carry a message to his real daughter.

He smiled to himself as he watched the bird fly far away. He knew his Perfect Princess would come to save him and take him home. It wouldn't be long now before he was rescued...

I tucked the page into a plastic pocket and clipped it into the big folder where I stored all of my story chapters. I'd been writing it ever since Dad left, and the bulging folder was getting hard to close. Even though there were so many pages in it, I knew every detail of the story and exactly how I wanted it to end.

The only thing I didn't know was what would happen next.

6

Jamie

"Jamie! I've told you a million times not to slam that damn door! I'm trying to work."

Chris sounds like he's had a bad day at the office. Which is bad for me too, since his office is our living room.

"Sorry!" I yell back at the top of my voice. I peel off my rain-soaked jacket and dump it on the floor along with my schoolbag and damp jumper. Leaving a trail of mud over the hall carpet, I race into the kitchen, forgetting in my frenzy to raid the fridge that I'm supposed to take my shoes off at the front door.

Mmm. Whipped cream in a can. Mum's been to the shops this morning.

I grab a couple of slices of bread and slather peanut butter and jam across them, shaking the whipped cream can and grinning at how much fun it is to scoosh it into big spirals on my sandwiches. Some of it goes over the counter, and some of it lands on the floor, but most of it goes on my bread, so that's OK. I stick another piece of bread over the top, double up my sandwiches and take a great big bite.

Mmm. Mad Jamie Specials. My favourite kind of snack.

"For God's sake! Do you have to eat like an animal?" Chris comes into the kitchen to refill his orange juice, and frowns when he sees the mess I've made. "Sit at the table – you're getting jelly all down your front." His American accent gets even stronger when he's on the verge of losing his temper. Right now he sounds like that singer Elvis Presley, so I know he's really angry with me.

"Sorry," I mumble through a mouthful of whipped cream, "I'll clean it up after." I won't though. We both know that in thirty seconds flat I won't even remember the mess exists.

Chris rolls his eyes and goes back to the living room to shout at his computer instead of me, and I bang the cupboards open and shut trying to find where Mum's hidden the cola this time. She doesn't like me having fizzy drinks, she says they make me even more hyper.

Aha! Behind the microwave. Bingo.

I slosh cola into a glass and wipe up the spillage with my sleeve, then I head upstairs while I'm waiting for Chris to finish work and stop hogging all the fun gadgets in the living room. Mum won't let me have a TV or a computer in my bedroom as I get way too obsessed watching shows or playing games, and then I get cranky and shouty when I have to stop and come out for dinner or go to school. It's not my fault watching horror films or playing *Zombie Attack 3* on the computer is way more exciting than real life.

I trip over a pile of laundry on my bedroom floor, and that reminds me that I'm supposed to take my school uniform off when I come home. I pull my shirt over my head so I don't have to waste time on the buttons, and drop it on the floor while I fish around under my bed for a top that doesn't have jam and cola stains on it.

Hey! What's that?

I forget all about getting dressed and grab the parcel that's sitting on my unmade bed. Chris must've left it there when the post came this morning. I don't need to read the Scottish return address. I already know it's from Dad.

I rip it open eagerly, wondering what he's sent me this time. I get a gift from him every week. 'Red Cross parcels' he calls them. He's never missed a single week since he moved out two years ago. He calls me every Sunday and Wednesday too, but the parcels are more exciting cos I never know which day of the week they're going to arrive. 'Bribery', Mum calls it, but she doesn't understand. He doesn't send me toys to buy my forgiveness for leaving us and moving in with his new family all the way up in Scotland. It's thoughtful stuff that no one else would think to buy me.

The brown parcel paper comes flying off, landing on the floor on top of my gym shoes. Dad sent me those a couple of months ago when I told him my old ones were giving me blisters in PE and Mum was too busy to get me new ones. Next to them is a big pile of pens, pencils, rulers, and a stack of Transformers notebooks and stickers. Dad got me all of them too. He knows I always lose stuff at school.

I hope it's the new smartphone with the fancy camera. *Please* say it's the new smartphone!

Dad said he'd get me one for going to the States so we could do video calls and I could send him pictures of my cool new school and fancy house and American Dream Life. I don't even know what that means, I just heard it on TV once, but I know it sounds better than the life I'm living now.

I'm so excited, I fight to get the bubble wrap off without checking if Dad sent the parcel by recorded delivery. There's *no way* he'd be dumb enough to send an expensive phone by ordinary post. He's clever, my dad, not like me.

There's only one vaguely neat place in my whole room, and that's the top of my chest of drawers where I've been piling all of Dad's 'Get Ready for Sunny California' gifts. I've got swimming trunks there, and surfer shirts. He sent me a specially made Transformers passport cover, and there's a journal where I can write down all the exciting things I do and see when I get to the USA. On top of that is a pair of supercool sunglasses and, so I don't forget home, a Southampton F.C. baseball cap, which is kind of a funny thing to call it since they're a football team. Just in case it gets cold in the winter, he's got me a beanie hat with 'Oakland Raiders' on it. That's the American football team from the new place I'm going to. Dad must've got that online specially too.

All I need now is the new smartphone, and I'm good to go.

I finally get the bubble wrap off, and stare at the box in disappointment.

It's not a smartphone. It's a chemistry set.

Usually a science kit would be a really good thing, and I'd be dead excited. Experiments are my favourite thing. Not the boring ones you do in school, I mean the kind where you mix things up and make them fizz and change colour and go boom, or grow insects in your bedroom and release them into the garden, or—

Uh-oh. The lid's come off my tank of ants again. I promised Mum I'd let them go outside as soon as I'd finished my experiment. Maybe if I look under my bed I'll be able to find them before she—

No! Focus. Figure out the mystery of the missing smartphone first.

Dad's always sending me new experiments to do so I can tell him what I've discovered when he calls. But why's he sending me a science kit when I'm going to California? It'll take up way too much room in my suitcase. I pick up the note and read it slowly.

Hi Sandwich Man,
Just a quick note as I'm running late and need to post this before my shift this morning. Sorry this isn't the smartphone, that'll need to wait a bit longer, as you probably know by now. We can do these experiments together, that'll be fun, won't it? Have you talked to your mum yet? Give me a call when you do and we can discuss what happens next.
Love, Dad x

OK, so that makes no sense. What does he mean, 'Have you talked to your mum yet?' Talked to her about what? Discuss 'what happens next'? Huh? That doesn't sound good. I know what happens next: I go to California and start a brand-new American Dream Life where I'm not a total headcase any more.

Just then I hear Mum walking down the hall and sighing over the muddy prints I've left on the carpet. Before I can hide my shoes so I can pretend it wasn't me, she knocks on my door.

"Jamie? We need to talk."

Ah. Looks like I'm about to find out exactly *what happens next.*

7

Elin

"Elin? Can we come in? We need to talk."

We?

Why did Mum always have to drag the Imposter into our family discussions like he was superglued to her and she couldn't peel him off? Mum came padding into my room in her socks, then Paul put his head round my door and came clomping in right behind her.

"A-HEM!" I cleared my throat loudly and glared at his feet.

"Oh, for goodness' sake, Elin!" Mum rolled her eyes. "He's wearing slippers. Can we just—"

"No, no, it's fine, I forgot. This is Elin's room, so it's her rules." Paul's smile was slightly strained as he went to take his slippers off at the door. He was always smiling. It was so annoying.

"It's a new carpet!" I said defensively when Mum wouldn't stop giving me *that* look.

"It's not new, it's over two years old."

"I want to keep it good."

"It's for *walking* on, Elin!"

"That doesn't mean—"

"Oh look! I haven't seen these before." Paul stepped right in with his size fifty feet and stopped our carpet discussion before it could turn into a full-blown argument. "Did you do these recently? They're really pretty." He picked up one of the plaster of Paris wishing pots sitting on my windowsill. Even though he was being really careful, it made the hairs on the back of my neck prickle angrily to see him touching it.

"I did them yesterday. Put it down please, the paint isn't dry yet."

That was a lie. Now I needed a truth to balance it.

"I'm going to give them to Gran for her birthday next Sunday."

"That's really thoughtful," Paul said, setting the little pot back down and checking he hadn't got any fingermarks on the paint. "I'm sure she'll love them."

How would you know? She's my dad's mum, not yours, and she's only met you a few times. She doesn't like you any more than I do.

Before Paul could start picking up any more of my fairy-tale figures I asked, "So… what did you want to talk to me about?"

I didn't really want to know.

There was a heavy knot of dread in my stomach that had been tangling up my insides for nearly a week, ever since Paul had got off the phone to his ex-wife and he and Mum had gone into her room and spent half the night whispering. Mum had red eyes at the breakfast table the next morning, but she said she was fine and just hadn't slept well. Now her eyes were big and wide and worried, just like they were the night she told me Dad was leaving.

Mum sat down beside me on my neatly made bed, and Paul

41

leaned against my desk, glancing at Mum nervously. I picked up my model of Athena and held her tightly for support, waiting for them to tell me the dreadful news.

Please-oh-please don't let it be another Mutant! I prayed, my eyes darting to Mum's stomach to check she wasn't swelling up like a balloon. I knew that was silly. Paul wasn't going to find out from his ex-wife down in Southampton that Mum was pregnant, was he? Anyway, Mum wouldn't inflict a pretend sister on me the way Dad had, not after I cried myself to sleep every night for a year when she was born.

But what if it was a half-step in that direction? What if they were getting *married*?

That would mess my family story up so badly I'd never be able to fix it, no matter how many fairy-tale versions I wrote.

"Elin, Paul and I have something we need to tell you," Mum began nervously.

I KNOW! Just get on with it.

"You know that Paul has a son your age who's living with his mum in Southampton?"

"Yes," I muttered through gritted teeth.

I knew all about Southampton. I'd heard *every* story about Mum's childhood there, how Paul had been her best friend since the first day of school, how she went to university up here in Glasgow and met Dad and married him instead, and how she and Paul were really soulmates who were meant to be together forever and ever, even though Paul had a family of his own down in stupid Southampton. Every time I heard her stories I wanted to punch the Imposter so hard he'd go flying through the air all the way back there. But instead of hitting Paul with my fists, I lashed out with my sharp tongue.

"You've told me about him," I snapped. "He's got something wrong with his brain and can't control himself, and he's been expelled from two schools already."

I held my breath, waiting for Paul's reaction to my mean words. That was the problem with trying to be perfect and in control all the time – I bottled up all my anger so tight that it turned to poison inside me, and when it leaked out it burned anyone it touched.

Paul's stupid smile slid right off his face, and his mouth opened and shut a couple of times. It was hard to tell whether he was angry or just upset. When he did manage to speak, his voice sounded all squeaky, like a balloon slowly deflating.

"There's nothing wrong with Jamie," he frowned. "He's not a bad boy, it's just…" Paul struggled to find the right words, and Mum jumped straight in to save him.

"The thing is, pet," she said, taking hold of my hand and giving it a squeeze, "there's been a change of plan. Jamie's mum has had to cope with a lot on her own for the last few years. She needs some time with her partner Chris, so we've decided it would be best if Jamie stayed with his dad for now instead."

"Oh," I said flatly, refusing to understand what she was telling me. "So where are you both going to live then?" I asked Paul.

He was all out of smiles now and was staring at the floor, wringing his hands awkwardly.

It was Mum who finally told me the horrible truth. I kept my eyes fixed on Athena the whole time she was talking, trying desperately to hold on to my beautiful fairy tale while all around me my world was collapsing. The big change Mum and Paul were going to make to our home life was going to spoil everything. If I let it happen without a fight then I'd never be able to get Dad back to live happily ever after with just me and Mum.

I finally put my hand up to make her stop and snapped, "That isn't going to happen! This is my home too, and you can't do it. You just can't."

"Look Elin, it's already been decided," Mum said more firmly. "It's not going to be easy, but we're a family now, and we have to work together. I'm sure you'll have great fun once—"

"NO!" I got up and marched to the door, waving them out like a traffic warden. "It's not going to happen, and that's final. I'd like to do my homework now, so please could you let me get on with it?"

That was a lie. My homework was already printed out and filed away in my schoolbag.

"Let's give her some time to get used to the idea, OK Liz?" Paul said softly to Mum, patting me on the shoulder as he put his slippers back on. "She'll come around."

The worried look Mum threw me said she wasn't so sure. She knew me *way* better than Paul ever would.

"I hate you," I whispered at Paul's back as I closed the door behind him.

Now the homework lie was balanced with a truth.

Jamie

"Don't come in, Mum! I'm totally naked!"

It's only a half-lie, as I'm only half-naked, but it suddenly occurs to me that the head teacher might've phoned Mum at work about my car-wrecking spree, and I'm about to be deep-fried in disapproval. My stalling technique might not be brilliant, but it's the best I can come up with in all of two-and-a-half seconds.

It doesn't work. Mum comes in anyway.

"Put a T-shirt on, Jamie," she sighs. "You're not a baby any more, you need to learn to dress yourself."

"I know how to dress myself," I huff, grabbing the nearest piece of clothing off the floor and pulling it on. "See? One arm. Two arms. Done!"

Mum heaves another sigh and I look down to see I've got my jam-and-cola-covered school shirt back on again. No biggie. I've got it on backwards so you can hardly see the stains anyway.

"Jamie, stop messing about, this is serious."

"I know it's serious. See? This is my serious face."

I plonk myself down, missing the edge of the bed and ending up sitting on a pile of clothes on the floor. "I'm really sorry, Mum. I didn't mean to nearly cause a pile-up on the road with that football, it was just a miskick, that's all. It could've happened to anyone. And no matter what Mr Patel says, I don't have it in for him, cross-my-heart-and-hope-to-die honest I don't. I wasn't even aiming those stones at his car, so he can't make you pay for the broken windows if it was just an accident, can he? And if the head teacher says I ran out of the school gates he's totally lying. The janitor was there and he wouldn't let me get past him, so I can't get suspended for breaking the rules if I didn't really break them, can I?"

I look up at her hopefully, but instead of being angry Mum just looks confused.

"Pile-up? Broken windows…? Jamie, did you get into trouble at school today?"

"Nope," I say without even thinking. "Uh-uh. No way."

"Right…" The way she's frowning I can tell she doesn't believe me, but there's something else she wants to say. She moves three cups, a plate covered in tomato sauce and a half-eaten bowl of cereal off my chair and sits down.

"Look Jamie, I know you don't like change, but sometimes things don't work out quite the way you plan them."

"Yeah, I know. Like I thought I was going to finish primary school in Mr Patel's class and go to the secondary school here, but now we're going to America instead. I know I get stressed about change, and I threw a big wobbly when you told me about it, but it's fine now, really. I've done loads of research on California, and I'm really looking forward to it. See?"

I point to the maps of America I've got pinned to the wall. I've scribbled bits of useful information that I found on the internet all over them. It's a lot of research considering I get all of five minutes at a time on the computer before Chris hogs it.

"Jamie, that's not what I meant." Mum runs a hand through her long brown ponytail, trying to find the right words to say, but I've already lost my focus. There's a stray ant from my tank crawling over my foot, and before I know what I'm doing I turn my foot over and crush it into the wooden floorboards.

Man-oh-man-oh-man! That was a mean thing to do.

I lift my foot and examine the squelched little blob on my big toe. Why did I do that? There's a churning in the pit of my stomach, and I feel like crying. That ant wasn't hurting anyone. I was supposed to be looking after it. Why did I kill it without thinking? Why can't I just THINK before I do something stupid?

"Jamie, are you listening to me?" Mum says again.

"Yes," I scowl, picking the squashed ant-ball off my toe and setting it on a dirty plate under my bed. I'll bury it in the back garden later, and as soon as Mum's stopped yakking at me I'll search my room for the rest of the escaped ants and let them all go free outside. That'll make me feel better.

"Jamie, this is important!" Mum is close to shouting now.

"I know! Change hard, America good, blah Blah BLAH! I KNOW!" I snap. I'm not angry at Mum, I'm angry at myself for killing that ant, and I want to get started rounding up the remaining ones before I die of guilt. I can't start searching till Mum's gone though, or she'll know I've left the lid off the tank and let all the ants escape. I glance at the shelf where the lidless

47

tank is standing like a great big 'I'VE GONE AND DONE A BAD THING AGAIN' signpost. Mum still hasn't noticed it. That'll be why she hasn't had a fit yet.

"… So you see why you can't go America? Why it's best for us if I go with Chris and you stay here with your dad?"

Yes yes yes, yack yack yack. Maybe I should get the magnifying glass from the forensics kit Dad sent me last Christmas. It's pretty strong, and if I use that and my Transformers torch I should be able to find all the ants that have disappeared under my…

Wait…

"WHAT?!"

My mouth hangs open, and Mum stops talking when she realises I've only just heard what she said. We stare at each other for a long moment, then her eyes slide to the floor and suddenly she's blinking back tears.

"I'm really sorry, but a fresh start is the best thing for all of us. I know you and Chris don't get on so well, and I want you to be happy more than anything. I just can't see the three of us making it work in America. You used to have such fun with your dad – wouldn't you like to live with him for a while instead of moving halfway round the world?"

She looks up at me and there's tears sliding down her face, and I want to brush them away and say it's all OK and slap her so hard at the same time I can feel my head about to explode.

"But-but-but…" I stutter like a faulty lawnmower that's swallowed too much grass. "But I HAVE to go to America! I have to go and get fixed, Mum! I can't stay here and be Mad Jamie the crazy freak any more, don't make me!"

"Jamie, we've talked about this," Mum says sadly. "Moving somewhere else isn't going to make your behaviour problems magically disappear. The doctors in America aren't any different from the ones here, and if Doctor Mackay says you need to work on controlling your temper and being more organised, then that's what the doctors in California will say too. And anyway, you *will* be having a fresh start. You'll go to live with your dad in Scotland, and that'll be fun, won't it? You're always saying you want to spend more time with him, so it's really a good thing, isn't it?"

She's sounding desperate now, but there's nothing she can say to stop my meltdown.

"But you PROMISED!" I'm gasping for breath, and my face is going so red my eyeballs are about to pop. "You PROMISED I was going to America!"

"Well you CAN'T go! Chris won't have it, so there's an end to it!" Mum tries to bite her tongue to swallow the words back, but it's too late.

"I HATE YOU! I hate you both! It's not FAIR!"

Before I can stop myself, I'm charging over to my stash of 'Get Ready for Sunny California' gifts and throwing them in every direction. The flying swimming trunks and surfer shirts knock over a glass of milk that's going sour on top of my bookcase, and smelly white liquid drips down onto my dog-eared collection of books. One leg breaks off the sunglasses as they smash against the wall, and the heavy journal shatters the plastic ant tank into a zillion pieces.

"Jamie! Stop it!" Mum cries.

But I'm not done yet. Not by a long way.

The maps of America are next. I tear them off my wall, ripping them into little bits and scattering the pieces over my bed. Then I grab the plate with the squashed ant on it and fling it against the wall so hard that dust flies up as it smashes. I stomp across the floor and start snatching milk-soaked books from their shelves, flinging them in every direction and howling at the top of my lungs. I've probably crushed half the escaped ants into the floorboards by now, and I can feel a bit of broken plate stabbing into my foot and drawing blood, but I don't care. I don't care about anything except how awful I feel and how unfair the whole universe is.

Mum's crying so hard it sounds like she's breaking, but I don't care about that either right now.

"This is why you can't come to America with us!" she yells with her hands over her ears to drown out my wailing. "I can't bear any more of this, Jamie. I CAN'T BEAR IT!"

She marches out and slams the door shut behind her so hard the whole wall shakes.

I drop to the floor and curl up in a puddle of sour milk and California surfer T-shirts I'll never ever get the chance to wear, and cry and cry until my throat's raw and my eyes are aching.

I don't want to be me any more. I don't want to be Jamie Lee, the mad bad boy who turns into the Incredible Hulk every time he loses his temper.

Maybe there's a better way to deal with all the anger and confusion and hurt that's boiling away inside me than shouting and raging and crying, but I have no idea what that is.

Destroying things is the only way I know how to manage my bad moods. But now I've gone and broken my family, and no amount of kicking and screaming is going to put it back together again.

9

Elin

"It isn't FAIR, is it Gran?" I wailed. "Mum promised I could start riding lessons for my birthday this year – she was saving up specially, and now she says we won't be able to afford them because of Paul's stupid son coming!"

"I know pet, it's a terrible idea." Gran patted my hand across the kitchen table. "From what your mother's told me he sounds like a right wee monster. How many schools has he been expelled from for bad behaviour? I don't know what your mother's thinking agreeing to this, it was really selfish of Paul to even suggest it."

Monster.

Yes, I liked that. 'The Monster' would be his name in my story from now on.

"Don't worry pet, I'll sort this out," Gran reassured me, piling more Jammie Dodgers on my plate and refilling my glass with Irn-Bru. "It isn't fair asking you to cope with more big changes after everything that's happened. If your dad was here today he'd agree with me."

"Why didn't he come, Gran? He's never missed your birthday before."

"Beth's still feeling poorly after her chickenpox. Sue couldn't get time off work, so he's staying at home to look after your wee sister instead."

"She's not my sister," I scowled. "I don't have a sister. And I *never* get to see Dad any more."

I looked forward to our once-a-month meeting at Gran's house in Whitburn more than anything. Now I'd have to go another whole month before I got a chance to see him again, and it was all the Wicked Witch and her mutant daughter's fault.

"You know, pet …" Gran began slowly, fiddling with her glasses the way she always did before she said something she knew I wouldn't like about dad's fake family. "Your dad would be happy to bring Beth over here if you'd just agree to meet her. That way you'd get to see him and …"

"No way!" I coughed, nearly choking on my Irn-Bru at the very thought of being in the same room as the Mutant. "That's not going to happen. You'd never let her come here Gran, would you? I mean, she's never been here before, has she?"

"I know you wouldn't like it, pet." Gran patted my hand again and gave me an encouraging smile. She was always on my side.

Always.

That was one of the reasons I loved coming back here, even though our old house was just down the road, and being here brought all the memories flooding back so fast I thought I would drown in them.

"Elin, would you do me a favour and nip down to the shops for some milk? I'm going to have a word with your mother," Gran said, fishing about in her purse for a five-pound note. That was her way of saying she was going to give Mum a piece of her mind about Jamie and she didn't want me overhearing the argument.

"Thanks Gran!" I called after her as she marched out into the garden, where Mum was clearing away the remains of the birthday barbecue. I put the money in my pocket and headed for the front door. I hated hearing adults yelling at each other, so I was happy for any excuse to get out of the way.

I took my time walking through the estate and down to the main road, where there was a row of shops and a post office. I didn't want to get back too soon, so I hovered round the magazine section in the corner shop, flicking through the comics until the woman at the counter started frowning at me. Mr Singh who used to own the shop didn't mind me reading the magazines back when we lived in Whitburn. It seemed like the longer I stayed in Glasgow with Mum and the Imposter, the less I belonged here. If I didn't get Dad and my old life back soon, all I'd have left of it was faded memories.

Instead of going back by the main road, I took the long way round, past the park and the small wood at the edge of the estate. I knew I shouldn't and it would only make me sad, but I couldn't help myself. It was like jumping in a time machine and going back to the past, only I ended up in some strange parallel world where everything was familiar but different. The park gate was padlocked and the abandoned slide was slowly rusting to death. The wood was overgrown and the council had cut down some of the trees.

Nothing was the same here any more.

Except…

Suddenly I stopped dead on the corner, staring at the house at the end of the road opposite. There, by the big field where the buttercups grew like a carpet of summer sunshine, was my fairy-tale castle.

The house still looked the same, with its red front door and green fence round the garden. But standing on the grass was a little boy holding a toolkit, watching while his father fixed stabilisers onto a bike. It brought back so many memories I wanted to sit down on the pavement and cry.

Dad taught *me* to ride a bike on that street. It was *me* who helped Mum choose the red door to match the flowers that grew by the front porch. Those were *my* family memories, and now another family had moved in and stolen them. I missed my old life here so much I felt sick. The thought of someone else living in my old bedroom hurt so much I wanted to scream.

I forced my feet to start moving again, counting to one hundred slowly to keep the hurt from turning into anger. I was scared if I let it out I'd start shouting with rage at the unfairness of it all, and never be able to stop. I'd heard Mum and Dad throw enough angry words at each other to last me a lifetime.

But I still couldn't escape them, even after the divorce.

When I got back to Gran's house I could hear her out in the garden arguing with Mum.

"This really isn't any of your business, Mary!" Mum's voice was getting louder, carrying all the way down the garden.

"Elinor is my granddaughter, and that makes it my business!"

Gran's polite voice was starting to crack at the edges, like a layer of ice. Gran had never really liked Mum, but she put up with her for my sake. Our visits usually ended up with them at each other's throats and me standing between them trying to be the referee. I could feel the Irn-Bru and Jammie Dodgers fizzing uncomfortably in my stomach as I listened to the shouting, so I did the only thing I could think of to make myself feel better: I tidied up and made things neat.

I folded all the glittery wrapping paper that Gran had taken off her presents, then I carried the three little wishing pots I'd given her into the living room and put them in the cabinet with the others I'd made her over the years. I'd whispered a wish into every one of them before I wrapped them up and gave them to Gran. It was the same wish every time.

"I wish I could have my family back again," I whispered. "My *real* family."

No more Fakes, Imposters, Mutants or Monsters, I thought. *Just me, Mum, Dad and Gran, like it used to be.*

"Please come true," I added, crossing my fingers for luck as I put the pots into the cabinet. I was just straightening the photos of me, Mum and Dad on the sideboard when I noticed a big photo album I'd never seen before hidden underneath the cabinet. It looked like a little kid had dipped the album in a bucket of glue then dumped a tube of glitter and a packet of cheap craft stars over the top.

Where did that *come from?*

Gran was my Fairy Godmother, and her house full of our family memories was my Enchanted Cottage. Nothing was ever out of place here, nothing was ever different. As long as everything stayed the same in this house, with my real family frozen in happy photos, then I could keep on believing that one day we'd all be together again.

This strange album didn't belong here any more than Dad's fake daughter did.

I was just pulling it out from under the sideboard to look inside when Gran's horrified voice cried, "Don't touch that!"

I dropped the album like it was on fire and gaped at Gran. She'd never raised her voice to me, not ever. She'd never had to.

"Sorry pet, I didn't mean to shout." Gran hurried over and took the album from me, putting it high up on top of the cabinet. "Those photos, they... er, they belong to a friend. I'm just keeping them for her. I promised I wouldn't let anyone touch them."

"Why?" I asked, feeling hurt at not being trusted. A part of me was a little ashamed too. I probably shouldn't have been poking about under Gran's cupboards. But it wasn't like she had any secrets to keep from me.

Did she?

"Um..." For the first time in her life Gran didn't have anything to say. Mum did though.

"Come on Elin, it's time to go. We have to pick that mattress up from the store before it closes or Jamie's room won't be ready for him coming."

It would serve him right, I thought darkly, dragging my heels all the way out to the car.

"You didn't manage to talk Mum out of it then?" I asked Gran as I gave her a big hug.

"No pet, I tried, but she and Paul are dead set on Jamie coming to stay. I don't like it any more than you do."

"Tell Dad I miss him."

"He misses you too, pet."

Just not enough, I thought sadly, blinking away real tears as I climbed into the car and Mum drove me back down the road to my fake dad and fake home in Glasgow.

Jamie

"It isn't FAIR, is it Aunt Cath?" I complain, kicking my feet against the back of her seat and forgetting she's already told me twenty times not to. "I don't want to go to Scotland. I don't want to live with Dad's girlfriend. I want to go with Mum to America."

Aunt Cath isn't really my aunt. She's my mum's best friend, and she's doing her a big favour driving me all the way up to Glasgow while Mum and Chris get the house clean and tidy for the estate agent coming to check it tomorrow. Mum needs to get her full deposit back, but we've been renting that house ever since Dad left, and I'm pretty sure I've had way too many plate-throwing meltdowns, wallpaper-ripping sprees and furniture-breaking binges for Mum to get a penny back. I did offer to help with the clean-up, but they said I'd get in the way. I think they just want rid of me as soon as possible.

"It's not fair that I can't go to America, is it?"

"Not this again, Jamie." Cath rolls her eyes at me in the rear-view mirror, which looks funny as it makes her face all back to front so her eyebrow ring is on the wrong side. "Just listen to your music, or play on my phone, OK? We're not even past Manchester yet, and I don't want to listen to you whining the rest of the way."

I stick my tongue out at the back of her head when she looks away again and pick up her phone, throwing it up and down and catching it until it falls on the floor. Then I have to go bin-raking under all the burger wrappers and sweet papers and empty plastic bottles I've thrown away so I can find it. It's like scuba diving in one of those giant landfill sites you see on the news, only this one's travelling up the motorway at seventy miles an hour and smells of sick. That's sort of my fault too. I shouldn't have had that second burger last time we stopped at the services.

"Jamie! Put your seat belt back on! How many times do I have to tell you?" Cath yells. Every time she looks back at me in the mirror her eyes get smaller and smaller, like they're shrinking. If I do anything else to annoy her between now and Glasgow her eyes are going to disappear altogether, and then how is she meant to drive, huh? Maybe I'll have to take over the wheel – I bet I could! I'd be just like one of those Formula One racers roaring up the motorway like I was in the Monaco Grand Prix.

Vroom, vroom! Watch out! Mad Jamie's about to overtake! Neeeurm! Vroom! SCREEE—

"Jamie! Stop making those silly noises! For goodness' sake, it's like driving with a chimpanzee in the back."

Cath's tried to be supportive of Mum and her problems with me over the years, but let's face it, she's never been my biggest fan. I've probably wrecked all chance of charming her by now though, what with spilling a supersized cup of cola all over her at the McDonald's outside Oxford, then nearly getting run over chasing a balloon that blew across from the fun fair on the other side of the motorway. She says she's not going to let me out of the car except to go to the toilet from now on, which is okey-dokey with me as I've already spent all the money Mum gave me for snacks on that teddy-grabbing machine at the Birmingham services.

I'd ask Cath for some more, but she's run out of pound coins. I already checked in her purse when she wasn't looking. Pity, I really wanted one of those Captain America soft toys too.

"Aunt Cath, can we stop? I need to pee."

"I told you not to drink the whole bottle of juice in one go! Wait till Manchester, we'll be there in half an hour."

"But that's too long! What if I can't hold it in? What if my bladder explodes? Please Aunt Cath, please! I really need to peeeeeeeeee—"

"JAMIE! That's enough! And stop bouncing up and down like that. You're eleven for goodness' sake, you can wait a little bit longer for the next stop."

I stop bouncing and start kicking the back of her seat again instead, trying to find something to take my mind off the two litres of fizz that's blown my stomach up like a balloon ready to pop. Cath isn't trying to be mean – she's stopped nine times for me already, and at this rate we'll never get to Glasgow before dark, even though she picked me up at the crack of dawn. We've been driving for hours and hours. We must be halfway across the universe by now. I'm bored boredboredboredbor—

Ooh, what's that?

There's something bright and shimmery on the road, with a billion colours dancing in the sunlight. It's like we're driving up a rainbow. Only there isn't a pot of gold at the other end, there's only Glasgow. At least my dad will be waiting for me there. I can't wait to see him again, even though I'm so nervous at the thought of moving to a new city with new people in a new house and going to a new school that I want to scream. I take my seat belt off again and press my face up against the window to get a better look at the swirling colours in the oil slick, trying to see past the sparkly diamonds of rain that are clinging to the glass.

The oil must be leaking from that big truck just up ahead. I really want to see the river of glittering colours up close, but the window's getting all fogged up and I can barely see out, and the truck's indicating to turn off the motorway at the next exit, and I'm not going to get a chance to see a melted rainbow on the road ever again if I don't do something quick…

So I do the one thing that'll give me a great view of the magical shimmering road before it disappears.

I open the passenger door.

There's a rush of wind, and before I know it the door's gaping wide and I'm clinging onto the handle with both hands, hanging out over the road and trying to pull myself back into the car with my feet. There's a screech of brakes and the loud honking of a horn in my ear as the car in the other lane swerves to avoid hitting me, and then Cath is shrieking my name and yelling her head off and our car is swerving too and we're lurching onto the hard shoulder and slowing down and the wind stops trying to tear me out and I finally close the door but the other one opens and Cath is standing there shouting Shouting SHOUTING!

"WHAT DID YOU THINK YOU WERE DOING?" I hear her roar through the fog of panic that's smothering me. My hands are shaking and I want to be sick again. The knot of moving-to-Glasgow dread in my stomach is now a giant ball of fear that I won't even make it there because I'm so stupid I'll get myself killed chasing rainbows on the road instead.

"You nearly fell onto the motorway!" Cath yells, like I hadn't already noticed. "God Jamie, what the hell is *wrong* with you?"

My throat's tight and I start sniffing. Before I can stop them, tears are pouring down my face and washing off the last little bit of sick and burger relish on my chin. It's not fair asking questions you already know the answer to. Cath *knows* what's wrong with me. Everybody does. I have ADHD, and that makes me Jamie the Freak-Boy who can't think ahead to work out just how dangerous opening a car door in the middle of a busy motorway is.

It's funny how just four letters can mean the difference between being normal and being the kind of monster whose own mother moves to a different country to get away from him.

"Are you OK? You didn't hurt yourself?"

When I can finally see through the blur of tears, Cath's face isn't angry any more, just really worried, and that makes me want to cry harder.

When we set off again she makes sure my seat belt's on and the doors are locked, and then she asks me to recite all the chemical elements from the periodic table and tell her what makes each one special. Soon I forget all about nearly getting killed, and

I spend the entire break at a pit-stop cafe near Manchester talking about oxygen. By the time we get to Carlisle I'm so busy describing the totally cool gas xenon, I don't even remember how much I'm dreading getting to Glasgow. Cath nods at me every now and then in the rear-view mirror to keep me talking as we head over the border. I think she's finally figured out that the only way to keep me out of trouble is to keep my mind occupied.

It's only when we pull into a big car park and I'm running out of things to say about radium that I realise it's dark and the street lights are on.

"Are we having dinner here?" I ask. I'm cheating too, cos I already know the answer.

"No Jamie, we're here. This is Glasgow. This is where we're meeting your dad."

Cath gets out of the car and goes to meet the dark-haired man who's already walking over to us with a big smile on his face. I press my own face against the glass and stare at him. The butterflies in my stomach have grown as big as helicopters, and it feels like they're all trying to take off at once. What if he's changed? What if he's different and he doesn't really want to be my dad any more? What if he's going to put me in an orphanage as soon as Mum's plane leaves? What if—

"Sandwich Man!"

Dad comes jogging over to open my door. I brace myself to endure a hug, but he doesn't hug me. Dad *remembers*. He puts his hand up for a high five, and I slap it in relief and give him a big grin too.

He hasn't changed a bit.

He's still my dad.

Cath doesn't remember though. She gives me a quick hug while I make a face at Dad behind her back that says, 'I hate this!' and he makes a face that says, 'Yeah, I know.' I pull away quickly and help Dad lift my suitcase into the boot of his car. Then it's time for me to go, and I'm getting nervous again at how new and different everything's going to be, and Cath turns to walk away and I almost don't want her to leave.

"Thanks for driving me here, Aunt Cath. Sorry I was so much trouble. Tell Mum I'll miss her."

"She'll miss you too, Jamie."

Yeah, just not enough.

I climb into the back of Dad's car and watch Cath drive off and leave me too.

"You ready, Jamie? You're going to *love* Glasgow. I know this is a big change, but it'll work out, I know it will. Give it some time – before you know it we'll be a proper family, you'll see."

At least I still have Dad. At least he still wants me. And maybe, if I try really REALLY hard to be good, his new family will want me too.

And that's what I want more than anything.

Part Two

Weaving Cocoons

Elin

"You should see what they've done to the spare room, Dad!" I said for the third time in as many minutes. "Paul's taken away all the nice guest stuff and covered everything in horrible football colours. It looks *awful*!"

"I know it's hard for you, Princess." Dad's voice was small and far away on the other end of the phone, like he was busy doing something else and not really paying attention. "But Jamie needs to feel at home there, and it *is* a spare room after all."

Dad didn't get it. I'd been keeping that spare room spotless for him ever since we moved here in case he came to visit and I got the chance to persuade him to stay for good. But he never came, he just kept saying it was too far and Sue was working and Beth needed to be looked after, and I should come and stay with them in Edinburgh for a weekend instead.

"But Paul's spent a *fortune* on all the stuff in there! And Mum's been going on for ages about how I can't have riding lessons yet as money's so tight. I was meant to get them for my birthday in a few months, but Paul's spending all the money on his son instead, and it isn't FAIR, Dad!"

"I'll have a talk to your mum about that," Dad said, sounding tired and distracted. That's what he always said when I mentioned riding lessons. Dad and Sue were spending all their money on Beth, and Mum and Paul were spending all their money on Jamie, and nobody seemed to have any money left to spend on me.

"And now Mum says he has to go to my school too!" I hadn't finished my list of complaints yet. "She filled in the paperwork for him to start on Monday, and she didn't even ask me if it was OK first! Why can't he go to another school, Dad? Why does he have to—"

There was a loud wailing sound from the other end of the phone that set my teeth on edge.

"I'm sorry Princess, Beth's just woken up from her nap, I'll have to go."

"But—"

"I love you. I'll see you soon, OK? Bye for now."

Dad disconnected the call before I could tell him I loved him back. Maybe that didn't matter to him now that he had a new, cuter version of me to fuss over. Everything was always Beth Beth Beth. I hated her so much I even made a wish in one of Gran's pots that she would be kidnapped by aliens and taken away to another planet.

"Elin, get off the phone, they're here!" Mum called from the kitchen before I could go and write a chapter of my story where the Mutant fell into the Wicked Witch's cauldron and was made into cabbage soup. I put Mum's phone back in her handbag and stomped down the hall.

Mum had stopped fussing with the pots on the cooker and was leaning over the sink to peer out of the kitchen window. There was a flash of lights in the dark as Paul's car pulled into the drive at the side of the house, then a slamming of doors and a crunching of feet up the gravel path. I ignored the sound of a key turning in the front door and started setting the dinner table slowly and carefully like I couldn't hear anything at all. Maybe if I pretended this wasn't happening the Imposter and the Monster would just magically disappear.

"Let's go and meet them," Mum said, turning the cooker down and hurrying into the hall. Her voice was too bright and her smile was too wide. She was nervous, I could tell. "Come on Elin, come and meet your stepbroth—" Mum managed to bite the word back before it slipped out, and changed it quickly to 'new friend' instead.

I don't have a stepbrother! I wanted to yell. *You're not married to Paul, so he's not my stepdad – I'll never call him that. I don't have a stepbrother or a stepdad or a half-sister or ANY OF THEM!*

There was just Mum and Dad and Gran and me, and we were surrounded by Monsters and Imposters who were trying to keep us apart. They weren't going to win – I was too clever to let anyone beat me. I'd been working on plans to make sure Jamie never settled in this house and would end up back with his mum. Plan A had been to keep my fairy-tale ending alive by talking Mum and Paul out of bringing Jamie here in the first place. Plan A had failed. It was time to move on to Plan B.

I set out the last cup, straightened the sauce bottles on the kitchen table, then went to join Mum in the hall. There was no avoiding it, I had to go and meet the enemy. I had to see exactly what I was up against if I wanted to win my real family back.

Plan B was war.

Jamie

This isn't what I was expecting.

I thought that Dad's girlfriend Liz and her daughter would just ignore me the way that Chris did. I wasn't expecting a big reception committee at the door.

"Hi Jamie, it's lovely to have you staying with us!" Liz smiles at me so brightly I'm blinded, and it takes me a minute to see there's a shorter version of her standing right behind her in the hall, scowling at me like I'm a big pile of dog poop that's just landed on her nice clean doormat. That's not the only thing that's clean in this house. Everything's so shiny white it's like I'm in an operating theatre. Dad might be a nurse, but he's never been *that* tidy. It must be Liz who's the clean freak around here.

The sick feeling in the bottom of my stomach gets worse when she gives me a big hug and I see Dad tense up like he's scared I'm going to react badly. I grit my teeth and try to smile at her, but all I can see is her super-neat short blonde hair and her perfectly ironed clothes that smell fresh out of the washing machine, and I know, I just *know* that I'm never going to fit in here.

"Elin, why don't you show Jamie round the house while Paul and I get dinner ready? We'll just be ten minutes."

The shorter version of Liz folds her arms and stares at me as Dad and Liz go into the kitchen. I'm not very good at reading people, and I'm not sure what she's thinking. I can tell when they're happy or sad, or angry or hurt, but that's about it. The scowl has gone and now this girl's face is blank, just like some creepy china doll sitting on the shelf in a haunted house, watching every move I make. I saw that in a film once. There was this guy who inherited a big old house from his great-grandmother, and when he moved in he found all these dolls that—

"Take your shoes off."

"What?"

The girl's still standing there looking at me.

"Don't say 'what', it's rude. Say 'sorry' or 'pardon'. Wipe your feet on the mat outside and then put your shoes on the rack in the cupboard here."

Elin's big green eyes follow me as I go back outside and wipe my feet on the mat, then take my shoes off and put them neatly on the rack she points out. Urgh. There is *no way* I'm going to remember to do *that* every day. I shrug my jacket off and go fishing around in my pocket for chewing gum, then I remember I used it all up in my failed attempt to break the world gum-chewing record on the way here. I always chew gum when I'm nervous, and this girl is making me all twitchy like I've got fleas in my underwear biting my bum.

"Seriously?" She says it so flatly I can't tell what she means.

"Um... what?"

"You're just going to fling your jacket on the floor and expect someone else to pick it up? What are you, a badly trained chimpanzee?"

"Oh, sorry…" I pick my jacket up again and hang it on the hook she points out in the cupboard. This is *not* going well. I don't think she likes me. "So… can I see the rest of the house?"

Elin looks me up and down, checking out the tomato-sauce stains on my T-shirt, the bit of chewing gum stuck to my jeans and my mismatched socks, then she jerks her head for me to follow her.

"Just don't touch anything," she sniffs.

She's got a long blonde ponytail that bounces against her back as she walks, and it's so silky and shiny-looking I'm tempted to reach out and grab it to see what it feels like.

DON'T. TOUCH. ANYTHING.

I stuff one hand into my jeans and the other into my mouth to chew my fingernails instead, following Elin round the house and trying not to wreck the place. I do pretty well. I knock over a plant in the living room and get soil on the carpet, and a big smudge of tomato sauce rubs off on the bathroom towels when I can't help feeling how fluffy they are, but Elin's too busy firing orders at me to notice.

"… And don't put the TV on in the evening when I'm trying to study, or in the morning, or… in fact, don't touch the TV at all without asking. Bathroom. Toothbrushes. Shampoo. Don't use anything in here without permission. Mum and Paul's room. Don't go in there. My room. None of your business. If you so much as touch my door handle, I'll kill you. The spare room. You're to sleep in here while you're staying with us, which probably won't be for very long. Any questions?"

"Um... so... do you like the Transformers?" I try, bouncing on my feet awkwardly and racking my brains for a way to make friends. Everybody likes the Transformers. They're the best thing ever. "You know – 'robots in disguise'." I hum the theme tune from the old cartoon I like to watch online.

"What?" The girl's eyes narrow to little black pinpricks.

"Don't say 'what'," I joke, "say 'sorry' or 'pardon'."

Elin's pupils disappear and all that's left of her eyes are huge circles of green that look like robot laser cannons ready to blast me out of existence.

"Elin! Jamie! Dinner time!" Liz calls from the kitchen.

I run back down the hall before the robot eyes can get me.

Maybe the Transformers aren't so cool after all.

13

Elin

This wasn't what I was expecting.

I chewed my chicken casserole slowly, staring at the boy opposite me as he bounced in his seat like a baby kangaroo and dropped bits of food in his lap.

For one thing, I thought he'd be bigger.

In my head the Monster was a giant – six feet tall and built like a tank. He had a shaved head and mean little eyes, with beefy fists ready to flatten anyone who got in his way. He was a loud-mouthed bully, a cartoon version of Rachel at school, and I was the hero who had to protect my family against him.

But Jamie wasn't any of those things.

He wasn't even as tall as me for a start.

He was small and skinny and full of twitchy nervous energy, and he talked so fast he sounded like a film playing at high speed. His dad's family were from Hong Kong, and Jamie's brown eyes and mop of black hair that flopped over his face when he talked made him look like the puppy version of Paul the Imposter.

He was the enemy, and I wasn't even scared of him. How was I meant to fight a war against a wimp like that? It was like trying to fight Beth for Dad's attention. She was so small and perfect there was no way I could win. Jamie looked like he'd fit right in here. He even had the same English accent as Mum and Paul. I was outnumbered at my own dinner table.

Jamie had a weakness, though. A big one.

He wasn't perfect like Beth. His ADHD meant he had trouble controlling himself. All I had to do was keep poking him to get a reaction and pointing out his faults until Mum realised what a terrible idea it was for him to stay here.

"Can you stop talking with your mouth full?" I interrupted him halfway through a long speech about his favourite video games before he could spit any more bits of carrot across the table. "I don't want to see your half-chewed food, it's disgusting."

Jamie stopped talking and shut his mouth tight, blinking at me like I'd slapped him in the face.

"He's just excited to be here, Elin," Paul said quickly. I could tell he was scared I was going to start an argument. He was right.

"But that's no excuse for bad manners, is it Mum?" I tried to get Mum on my side, but it didn't work very well. She hesitated, then smiled a big fake smile at Jamie.

"Would you like some more casserole? There's more in the dish on the cooker. I'll just—"

"I'll get it!" Jamie jumped up and dashed across the kitchen before Mum could finish.

"Wait Jamie, it's hot! Don't—"

"OW!"

Jamie burned his hand trying to pick the casserole dish up and the whole thing crashed to the floor, spraying chopped carrot, chicken and gravy all over the freshly mopped tiles.

"Are you OK, son?" Paul hurried over and ran Jamie's hand under the cold tap before Mum could react.

I knew exactly what I had to do. I rolled my eyes at Mum and went to fetch paper towels and the mop, whispering to her as I passed, "He doesn't listen, does he? That's why he's always in trouble at school."

"It was just an accident," Mum whispered back. But her eyes went to the floor, where the casserole she'd spent hours making lay in a sorry squelched heap, and I could see she was biting her lip to keep her real feelings hidden.

"You need some help there?" Paul asked me when he'd finished making sure Jamie hadn't burnt his hand off.

"No thank you, I can manage." I never let Paul help me with anything. I didn't want him thinking I needed him around.

"Why don't you make us dessert, Jamie?" Paul said, trying to lighten things up again. "I bought jam and cream, so you can make us a batch of your Sandwich Man Specials."

Jamie was still sniffing and cradling his hand like he was scared it was going to fall off, but his eyes suddenly lit up. He rushed to the fridge and started pulling out jam and a can of whipped cream as if he owned the place.

"Hey Elin, you want to try my sandwiches?" he asked as he flung pieces of bread onto plates and started slopping on so much peanut butter he used up half the tub.

"No thank you," I said frostily. I didn't want Jamie doing anything for me either.

"You'll like these," Paul winked at me and Mum. "No one can resist one of Jamie's special sandwiches."

I could, and I was pretty sure Mum could as well. Her polite smile had faded, and her mouth was now a flat line as she watched Jamie getting jam all over the freshly scrubbed worktop and whipped cream on the floor. Ever since Dad left, Mum had been much fussier about keeping the house neat. I helped out a lot with the cleaning too, doing the laundry after school, and hoovering the whole house. Maybe if there hadn't been so many arguments about the mess before, Dad would still be here instead of Paul and his stupid son.

Mum was ready to tell Jamie off. All I had to do was stir a little bit harder and he'd be in trouble.

"Jamie!" I rolled my eyes in an exaggerated circle. "I just cleaned your casserole mess off the floor. Now I'll have to clean your jam and cream mess up too. Could you stop spraying food everywhere?"

"Elin, the casserole was an accident, and this is just a bit of fun," Paul frowned. "We'll clean it up in a minute."

"Elin's right, Paul." Mum stood up and grabbed a cloth from the sink and started wiping down the cupboard doors that were covered in blobs of whipped cream. "Jamie, that's enough cream, it's going everywhere. Next time use a spoon for the jam, you're getting it all over the floor with that knife."

A flicker of annoyance crossed Paul's face. It was the first time I'd ever heard Mum contradict him, and the first time I'd ever seen him bothered by anything she'd said.

Good. I smiled to myself as I dumped the last of the casserole in the bin.

The war had begun.

14

Jamie

Elin doesn't like me.

She didn't even try my Mad Jamie Specials, and they're my best thing.

Maybe if I give her my Transformers torch she'll be my friend. It's my best thing too, but if it'll make her stop looking at me like I'm a monster then she can have it.

I'm rummaging around in my backpack to look for it when there's a knock on my door and Dad comes in.

"Going to bed already? I thought you'd want to stay up and watch a film. You haven't seen the new Star Trek one yet, have you?"

Dad knows all my favourite things, everything I've ever watched or read, all the science experiments I've ever done, all the food I like to eat and what music I like best. He sometimes even knows what I want for Christmas before I've decided myself. He knows me better than anyone on the planet.

The only thing he doesn't know is how much I hate it here and how much I want to go home to Mum.

"I'm tired," I lie. I don't like lying to Dad so I add, "It was a long drive up, and it nearly killed me." That bit's true, at least. I give a fake yawn and pat the Southampton F.C. quilt on my bed. "Thanks for the football stuff." I know that was Dad's idea.

"I wasn't sure what team you'd like up here – most people go for Rangers or Celtic, but that's up to you. When you decide who to support we'll start going to matches like we did in Southampton, OK?"

"Yeah. That sounds good."

Dad's trying really hard, so I give him a big smile when he sits next to me on the bed, even though I'm feeling so sad my whole chest is aching with the effort not to cry.

"I was going to get a TV for in here, but I thought you'd like to pick one yourself. I'm taking the day off work tomorrow so we can go and do a bit of shopping together, would you like that?"

That makes me smile for real. Mum never let me have a TV in my room. Dad's way less strict.

I usually hate shopping. Supermarkets are full of distracting smells and noises and things to touch, and every time I go out with Mum I end up having a meltdown by the time we get to the checkout. Unfamiliar places make me really nervous, but as long as I'm out with Dad I know it'll be OK. Even if I have a major freak-out he won't be mad at me. Dad's always on my side.

Always.

"Look Jamie, I'm really sorry about America. Your mum and Chris are still getting to know each other, and they just need a bit of time together on their own. It's not that your mum doesn't want you around any more, don't ever think that, OK?"

"OK," I say automatically without really meaning it.

"When I moved to Scotland, we didn't lose touch, did we? We're still friends, hey Sandwich Man?" Dad nudges me and I nudge him back, and then we have an elbow fight that only ends when I fall off the edge of the bed.

"Is everything alright in there?" Liz calls from down the hall. I think she's worried that I might be wrecking the house already.

"We're just horsing around," Dad calls back. "I'll be down in a minute."

That makes me laugh. He can't go down – there's no downstairs in this house, everything's one level. It was our old home in Southampton that had upstairs bedrooms. I think Dad's forgotten which house he's in for a moment.

He helps me straighten my quilt and find my pyjamas in my suitcase, then he switches the lamp on and turns off the main light.

"Night, son. I'll see you bright and early for that shopping trip, yeah?"

"Yeah," I nod, struggling to get my T-shirt off. This one's got casserole on it as well as jam. I'm like a one-man walking vending machine. They could start serving my T-shirts up in fancy restaurants as five-star cuisine. I could get my own cooking show where I fling food over myself and then get Gordon Ramsay to give it marks out of ten. I could have roast beef t-shirts and chocolate cake T-shirts and—

"Dad!" I call, just before he closes the door. I nearly forgot to ask him the question that had been burning me up all the way here.

"What?" He sticks his head back round the door.

"Can they fix me here? Can the doctors here in Scotland make me normal?"

I'm not good at reading people, but I can read Dad. Right now he looks really sad.

"Jamie, there's nothing wrong with you, you're fine just the way you are."

But I'm not though. I'm broken and splintered and I hurt people on my jagged edges. I was going be a normal boy in California. That was my American Dream. I know the doctors there must have a cure for my ADHD, I mean, they have *everything* in the USA – baseball and monster trucks and hotdog stands and living it up in Las Vegas.

That's all just a big broken promise now.

I pull on my pyjamas and climb into bed, tucking my Transformers torch under my pillow and turning off the lamp. In the dark, my fake smile falls off and I start crying.

If I can't go to America and become a whole new and improved me, then there's only one thing I want to do.

I want to go home.

15

Elin

This war wasn't going to be as easy to win as I first thought.

It was quarter to eight on Monday morning, and I was so tired I could barely keep my eyes open. Jamie had been here less than a week, and already he'd turned the whole house upside down. If he stayed here much longer I was going to die of exhaustion, and not just from spending all my time cleaning up after him.

"Did you get much sleep last night?" Mum asked, yawning into her coffee as she frantically re-typed her office report. She'd finished it on Saturday, but last night Jamie had been mucking about on her laptop without asking and accidentally deleted a whole bunch of files. He was always touching other's people's stuff without permission and breaking things. It was driving me and Mum crazy.

"How could I sleep?" I moaned, arranging the cheese slices carefully on a pile of bread for our packed lunches. "Jamie was up all night again! Can you get Paul to take that TV out of his room Mum, please? He had it on at four in the morning, and he was in the bathroom for over an hour just playing with the taps.

I'm never going to be able to stay awake in school. When's he going home?"

"We've talked about this, Elin," Mum sighed. "He's Paul's son and this is his home now too. He's just taking a bit of time to settle in, that's all. It'll get better."

"When?"

Mum didn't have an answer for that. She just frowned and went back to bashing the keys on her computer.

By the time it was ten past eight her report was done, and I'd finished loading the washing machine and tidying up the kitchen. Mum made me keep a bowl and a box of cereal out for Jamie, but if it was up to me he'd be going to school hungry. It wasn't fair that he kept us up all night then wouldn't get out of bed in time for breakfast. He was so selfish.

"Jamie!" Mum called down the hall for the millionth time. "I'm leaving in ten minutes. If you're not ready you won't get a lift to school and you'll have to go and meet your new teacher on your own."

There was a loud thump from Jamie's room as he went banging about, and five minutes later he finally emerged, yawning and licking off the felt-tip pen marks he'd somehow managed to get all over one hand. He slumped down at the kitchen table and began eating Honey Flakes out of the cereal box, examining his face in his spoon like it was the most fascinating thing he'd ever seen.

"I told you to get dressed!" Mum rolled her eyes when she saw what he was wearing.

Jamie looked down at his pyjamas in confusion. "I *am* dressed."

"I meant put your school uniform on! I told you to lay it out on your chair for this morning. Elin, help him find it, I'm going to be late for work at this rate."

"He's not a baby! Why should I—"

"Just do it Elin, please! Paul couldn't get time off work, and one of us has to take Jamie into school on his first day. I've got a big meeting this morning and I need to be out of the house in five minutes."

"Fine!" I muttered, grabbing Jamie by the arm and dragging him back down the hall.

"Hey! I haven't finished breakfast!"

"Then you should've got up earlier, shouldn't you? Mum's going to be late for work, and I'm going to be late for school. Stop being so selfish and get your stupid clothes on. Where are they?"

I gazed round the wreck of our spare room in dismay. A few weeks ago it had been ready for the visit from Dad I'd been dreaming about. Now it was a total nightmare. Clothes were strewn all over the floor, the football quilt was strung over two chairs to make a tent, and there was a greasy layer of empty crisp packets and snack wrappers covering every surface. On the table in the corner was a long rack of test tubes with funny-smelling liquid inside, and the TV was blaring even though Jamie had been warned not to switch it on in the morning. Mum said we needed to give him space, so she hadn't come in here with a hoover all week. If she knew the toxic health hazard he'd turned our nice clean spare room into she'd go ballistic.

"Where's your uniform?" I demanded, pulling the quilt off the chairs and searching for his shirt.

"Um…" Jamie went fishing around in his sea of clothes and finally came up with a creased shirt and a pair of new trousers that had an ink stain on them already. "Got them! Er… You're not going to stand there and watch me get dressed, are you?"

"You've got thirty seconds before I come back in." I closed the door and drummed my fingers on the other side so he could hear me counting down. When I opened it again Jamie had at least managed to get his trousers and his shirt on, but his socks and his school shoes were nowhere to be found. As we searched though the piles of discarded clothes and tangled bed sheets, I started to panic. I'd never been late for school in my life. Would Miss Morrison be angry with me? Would she give me extra homework? Would my perfect record be ruined? This was all Jamie's fault!

"That's it, we're leaving right now." Mum was at the door, tight-lipped and pale-faced. "Get in the car. I've only got time to take you as far as the park or I'll hit the worst of the traffic. I'm really sorry Jamie, but Elin will have to take you into school and introduce you to your new teachers."

"I can't go to school," Jamie wailed, sounding like he was about to cry. "I've only got one shoe, look!" He held up the black school shoe he'd found behind the curtain on the windowsill. "I can't go to school with just one shoe, can I?"

That was when I realised what he was up to.

He was doing this on purpose. He was trying to make us so late that Mum would just leave him behind. It was the dumbest plan ever, and I was so mad at him I wanted to clobber him over the head with his one shoe.

"Then put your trainers on. They're in the hall cupboard. Elin, can you get his schoolbag and—"

"His schoolbag's here and the lunchboxes are sitting by the front door."

"Good girl. Let's go."

We waited on the front step as Jamie went banging about in the cupboard for his trainers and jacket. He took so long I thought he'd wandered off into Narnia.

"I'm starting the car now!" Mum warned, rattling her keys. "If you're not out in ten seconds there'll be no TV for a week."

"Wait! I need to get my Transformers torch! I can't go to school without it," Jamie yelled as he ran back down the hall to his bedroom. "Just hang on a second…"

"Jamie, for goodness' sake! Will you just DO AS YOU'RE TOLD!"

Jamie

They think I'm being bad on purpose.

They've got no idea how hard it is for me to stay focused long enough to get easy things done, like putting on my school uniform or brushing my teeth after breakfast. My mind goes off in twenty-five directions at once and I'm always left behind. If you add in the stress of something new and scary like starting a different school, then it's like one of my science experiments has gone wrong inside my head and my brain's about to explode and come fizzing out of my ears. I'm so scared I want to throw up the seven-and-a-half Honey Flakes I managed to choke down this morning before Elin made me go and get my uniform on.

My stomach is churning and burning and flipping and flopping and—

"Jamie, will you please STOP kicking my seat!"

That's the fourth time Liz has told me off. Her eyes are green instead of brown like Aunt Cath's, but in the rear-view mirror they've gone just as small and angry.

I wish Dad was driving me to school.

He knows the best way to stop me kicking the seats is to let me sit in front. Elin's hogging the front seat though. She's worse than Chris with the fun stuff in Mum's living room when it comes to sharing anything. If Dad had been here this morning instead of going to work at six then I wouldn't be so scared. I can't think straight when I'm scared. Chewing gum helps me calm down, but I finished my last packet before breakfast.

This is all so new and strange. I hate it, I Hate it, I HATE it!

I want to go home.

"Right, I'll need to let you two out here." Liz stops the car at a line of trees by a park and turns in her seat. "Sorry I can't take you all the way, but I need to get to work on time. The school's expecting you though Jamie, so don't worry, it'll all be fine."

I think she can see just how worried I am, cos her eyes have gone soft again and she's trying to give me an encouraging smile.

"Elin will help you find your way round, won't you?"

Elin throws me a look that I'm pretty sure means she'd rather see me drown in a tragic washing-machine accident than help me, but since I'm not so good at reading people I hope I've got that wrong. I get out of the car reluctantly, and Elin gives me another funny look, grabbing my schoolbag and lunchbox from the back seat before Liz can speed off.

"Can't you remember anything?" Elin mutters. "Here, carry them yourself, I'm not your slave. Come on, we're going to be late."

"OK! I'll race you."

"Jamie! STOP!"

Elin's cry is drowned out by the screech of car brakes as I

run across the road without looking, and a taxi skids to a stop. One more second and I'd have been a big blob of blue school uniform and brand-new shoes squelched into the tarmac. Elin comes running over to grab my arm and drag me onto the pavement. Her face is bright red as she apologises to the taxi driver, who's yelling something my mum would ground me for a month for repeating.

"What is *wrong* with you?" she snaps, squeezing my arm like a tube of toothpaste. I'm SO tired of hearing that question.

"I've got ADHD," I say in a small voice. "Dad told you and Liz all about it."

"I don't care! It's no excuse for acting like a complete lunatic!"

It sort of is. That's the whole point of having letters after your name. So people know whether you're clever like Doctor Mackay MD or ADHD crazy like me.

"Oh no! That's the bell!"

There's a distant ringing sound coming from behind a row of houses, and Elin's face goes from red to white in the space of about three seconds.

"We're going to be in so much trouble! Miss Morrison always gives latecomers extra homework. Come on Jamie, we have to run!"

"Just a second, I need to tuck my shoelaces in."

I'm shoving my laces down the side of my trainers for the billionth time when I see it. There in the garden up ahead is a shiny new football sitting just out of reach behind a hedge. Before I can stop myself, I've clambered over the gate and grabbed it, stuffing it into my school bag and jumping the gate again so quick you'd have to slow time down to see me.

"What are you *doing*?" Elin gasps. "You can't steal things from people's gardens!"

"I'm not stealing it, I'm just borrowing it till home time. I'll put it back. Promise."

I bet the other boys in my new class like football. I bet if I bring one to school they'll all want to be my friend and play with me at break time. Maybe I'm not completely crazy after all. Maybe I'm a genius!

But by the time we get to the school gate my confidence is gone and I'm biting my lip and squeezing my hands into fists so hard my fingers are aching.

"Now what?" Elin tries to pull me into the empty playground with her, but this time I stand my ground.

"You go, I'll wait here till home time. We can just pretend I went to school today, OK?"

"Don't be so stupid! If you don't move RIGHT NOW then I'm going straight to the head teacher and he'll call the police and then you'll have to do as you're told or you'll be expelled before you've even started and your dad will be so mad at you he'll throw you out, and your mum doesn't want you so you'll end up in a home for bad boys and you'll spend the rest of your life in jail and—"

"STOP IT! Just STOP IT! I can't take this!"

I always wanted to be a Transformer, a superhero who went from fast car or jet plane to cool crime fighter in five seconds flat. But I'm not, I'm the Incredible Hulk, and when I get mad or scared I lash out and hurt people. Elin's standing too far away, so I hurt myself instead. I kick the school gate so hard my foot feels like it's breaking, but I keep on kicking it and hitting it and shouting till the buzzing sound of angry bees in my head is gone and all I'm left with is a big empty space where happy thoughts of a new life in California should have been.

Elin

By the time Jamie calmed down and started acting like a semi-normal human being again it was half past nine and I was so stressed I felt sick. The school playground was silent, and the only sound was Jamie's heavy breathing as he hung onto the gate.

"Are you OK now?" I asked warily, edging closer like he was a butterfly I was trying to trap in a net.

Jamie gave one last sniff and nodded. He looked exhausted. I almost felt sorry for him, till I remembered Miss Morrison and her extra homework.

"Right then, let's get going."

I grabbed his sleeve and held onto it tightly, marching him to the front door and pressing the buzzer. All the doors were locked now. The office staff would have to let us in.

"Hello? It's Elin Watts from Primary Seven. Can you open the door please?"

The lock gave a loud click and I dragged Jamie inside, not willing to let him go for a second till I'd delivered him to the head teacher.

"You're late today," the secretary frowned as we passed her office. "Is everything OK?"

"It's fine." I gave her one of my innocent smiles and made a mental note that I'd have to balance that lie with a truth sometime later today.

I could feel Jamie's arm trembling in my grip as I knocked on Mr Conway's door, and when I glanced at him he was all huddled up in his jacket like a caterpillar trying to hide inside its cocoon. It was hard to stay angry at someone who looked so frightened. I knew exactly how he felt. I could still remember my first day here, and how scared I'd been going to my new class where I didn't know anybody.

"Hey, it's alright," I said without thinking. "Our head teacher's nice, there's nothing to be worried about."

I bit my lip. I didn't want Jamie to think we could ever be friends.

"Come in. Ah, Elin, you're very late, that's not like you. And this must be your stepbrother Jamie. I was wondering where you'd got to." Mr Conway frowned at me but gave Jamie a welcoming smile.

I bit my lip even harder, all my sympathy for Jamie disappearing in a flash. He wasn't my stepbrother, he was the Monster, and if my story was ever going to have a happy ending, then the Monster had to be defeated. And that meant I couldn't ever let myself feel sorry for him. I let go of his arm and stepped back.

"Can I go to class now, Mr Conway?" I asked, ignoring Jamie's attempts to hold onto the edge of my jacket to stop me leaving him.

"Or do you need me to take Jamie to Mr Robertson's room?"

"Ah... Hold on just a second Elin, there's been a bit of a change of plan. Class numbers you see – we're not supposed to go over thirty, and Mr Robertson's already teaching thirty-one."

As he shuffled the papers on his desk, his words set every hair on the back of my neck prickling.

I thought nothing could be worse than Jamie coming to live with us.

I was wrong.

The worst thing that could happen was Jamie being put in my class where he could embarrass me in public.

My feet were heavy with dread as I followed Mr Conway down the corridor to Miss Morrison's room. How was I supposed to keep my perfect reputation in one piece with Jamie the Monster causing havoc in my class? Rachel and Lauren were going to make my life hell when they realised how much fun they'd have winding me up about him.

I can't believe this is happening! I thought, feeling my fairy-tale life slipping even further out of reach. *This is a total nightmare!*

"We're very big on discipline here, Jamie," the head teacher said as he marched down the corridor with one hand on Jamie's shoulder. I wasn't sure if he was trying to be reassuring or making sure Jamie didn't make a run for it, but it just made things worse, as Jamie kept trying to twist away from his hand like he was being electrocuted.

"We like to keep a peaceful working environment in this school, so that should help you stay focused."

Jamie's eyes were darting in every direction like he was

a chameleon who could look two different ways at once. They followed the tootling of recorders from the music room, the muffled shouts of the dodgeball players in the gym hall, and the chanting of poetry being recited in one of the classrooms. From the bewildered look on his face I could tell Jamie didn't agree with Mr Conway's definition of 'peaceful'.

"Right Jamie, here we are, 7B. You'll be in Miss Morrison's class with Elin. She'll help you settle in, won't you Elin?" Mr Conway smiled. The weak smile I gave him back felt more like a grimace.

The Dragon came striding out of her lair to glower at us both, and I could feel myself shrivel up under her disapproving glare as she talked in a hushed voice with the head teacher. Mr Conway whispered something about 'budget cuts for additional support' and how he'd 'try to rearrange the classroom assistants' timetables', then he smiled at us again and left us in the Dragon's clutches.

"Go and get your maths books out Elin, you're very late," Miss Morrison snapped. My face turned red with embarrassment again as I hurried to my table, trying to avoid the stares and sniggers from the rest of the class. "There's a spare seat at the back here, Jamie. Write your name neatly on your jotter and turn your maths book to page seventeen. I'd like you to do a bit of revision before you join one of the maths groups."

I heaved a sigh of relief. At least Jamie wouldn't be sitting anywhere near me.

I checked the board to see what page my group was doing today, then grabbed my textbook from my tray and set to work. I would have to finish this in double-quick time to prove I was still perfect.

Even though I was exhausted from Jamie's noise keeping me up all night, I still managed to hand my book in before the rest of my table. The next activity was to continue our Viking stories, but as I'd done mine already I had ten minutes of free time before break.

Finally! A chance to escape from Jamie's madness, Miss Morrison's disapproval and Rachel's sniggers, and disappear into dreamland. It wasn't long now till my birthday, and I had a party to plan. It was going to be the best one ever. I pulled my birthday book from my schoolbag and put the finishing touches to the picture of the amazing castle cake I wanted Mum to get me. It had three layers and was covered with pink icing, with four turrets and—

Suddenly a ball of scrunched-up paper hit me on the side of the head. I looked up to see Rachel and Lauren trying to get my attention across the table. My throat went dry. I couldn't ignore the two bullies, but Miss Morrison and her stack of marking was only ten feet away. I didn't want to get caught talking.

"So, are we getting an invitation then?" Rachel whispered, pointing to the birthday book that I'd been trying to hide from view with my arm.

"To what?" I tried to pretend I didn't know what she meant.

"To the *party*," Lauren hissed. "We're coming, right?" Her voice was too loud and Miss Morrison glanced up sharply. We all put our heads down like we were working, and when she went back to marking again Rachel whispered, "You *are* going to invite us to your birthday party next month, *aren't* you?"

"Um…"

No, I wasn't. There were thirteen other girls in the class, and I'd been planning to invite ten of them. I didn't want Rachel or Lauren or Paige Munro anywhere near my house.

"I didn't think you'd want to come," I lied, squirming with embarrassment. I was doing that a lot today.

"Of course we do! You *are* going to invite us, right?" It wasn't a question. Rachel was giving me an order.

"Er… I suppose—"

"Elin, if you've quite finished having a chat, then could you get some work done today please? There are a lot of silly mistakes in your maths book. A little concentration from you would go a long way." Miss Morrison was frowning at me over the top of her glasses.

"Ooh, little Miss Perfect's in trouble!" Lauren sniggered when Miss Morrison looked away.

"I think she's going to cry!" Rachel whispered loud enough for the other kids at our table to hear. The laughter got louder, and my cheeks felt like they were on fire, but then I realised it wasn't me they were all looking at. Everyone was turning in their seats to stare at the boy at the back of the class who'd wandered over to the project corner and was pulling tubes of glitter out of the art tray. Jamie was shaking them out into his hand and letting the glitter run through his fingers, watching it sparkle in the sunlight as it fell to the floor. He looked like he was lost in his own world, too absorbed in his own thoughts to notice that the whole class was watching him.

Miss Morrison put her red pen down with a thump and went marching across the classroom. The laughter at each table stopped the instant she swept past, and everyone held their breath. It was strange, but part of me didn't really want to see Jamie getting into trouble. After all, it was his first day and he was scared. It wasn't as if he was bothering anyone or making any noise.

Don't be so soft! I heard the voice inside my head say. *He's the enemy and we're at war! The quicker Jamie gets expelled and goes back to his mum, the quicker you'll get rid of Paul and get your real family back.*

That's right – Jamie was the enemy. I mustn't forget it no matter how pathetic he looked standing there crying while Miss Morrison shouted at him.

"This is maths time – does that look like the maths tray to you?"

"No…" Jamie gulped and wiped his nose on his sleeve, smearing glitter across his cheek.

"I know you have problems concentrating, but that's no excuse to disturb everyone else. One of the classroom assistants will be here after break to help you, but in the meantime, I need you to sit down and get some maths work done without any more fuss, understood?"

I put my head down and got on with my work. I didn't want to watch Jamie getting shouted at any more. Miss Morrison didn't sound like she had much sympathy for Jamie and his ADHD.

From now on, he certainly wasn't going to get any from me.

18

Jamie

"What you wearing glitter for? Do you think you're a My Little Pony or something?"

The other boys all laugh and I laugh too, though I'm not sure what's so funny. Making friends is hard, and break time is even harder for me than class time. At least when we're in class there are rules I can learn, even if I forget them half the time. Out here in the playground it's like the Wild West and I'm the stranger everyone wants to run out of town.

"So, do you want to play football? I brought a ball." I show them the brand-new one I borrowed from the garden down the street.

The boys look more interested now. They nudge each other and whisper, and then Steven says, "OK. You're in goal though."

I think Steven's the leader, so I'd better do as he says if I want to be in his gang. Being in goal's A-Okay by me, as long as I get to join in.

I run over to the goal at the end of the pitch and kick the ball out really far to show I'm not completely rubbish, but before the game can even start Darren's picked the ball up and is examining it like it's one of those Rubik's Cube puzzles he's trying to figure out.

"Hey Steve, isn't this your ball? The one you got for your birthday?"

Uh-oh…

Steven jogs over to look at it, and his eyes go wide like he's just solved the puzzle.

"That's the Rangers sticker I put there, right under my initials! Hey, you wee thief, where did you get this?"

All the boys are staring at me and I know I should tell the truth and say I was going to put it back at home time, but my brain's not working right and I'm scared, so I blurt out the very first thing that flashes into my head.

"It's mine. My dad gave it to me."

"Liar!"

"You *stole* it from Steve!"

"What the hell is wrong with you, you wee *freak*!"

That's it. I can't take the stress. Time to go.

Their shouts follow me the whole length of the pitch as I take off, running as fast as I can. I don't know where I'm going, I just know I have to get away before I blow up. Everything here is new and strange and scary, so I look for the one person who's even vaguely familiar and safe.

I look for Elin.

She's sitting by herself on a bench writing in her birthday book. I know it's her birthday book cos I found it in her desk drawer when she was hoovering the living room last night. I didn't mean to go into her room, honest I didn't. I just sort of stumbled into the door handle on the way back from the bathroom and the door sort of slid open and I sort of got lost trying to find my own room.

Sort of.

Her room's so super-neat it's scary, and all those hand-painted princesses and knights are amazing and kind of creepy all at the same time. I didn't mean to touch any of them, but I might have accidentally chipped one of the mermaids when I dropped it. It was just a tiny crack though.

I hope she doesn't notice.

I didn't mean to poke around in her desk either, but I really needed a pen to write down a new science experiment I'd just thought of. The book was hidden under a bunch of school folders, and I only opened it to check if there was a pen inside, but instead there was all this cool stuff about her birthday party next month and how she's planning to have a castle cake and get horse-riding lessons, and there was a list of all the people she's going to invite. I added my name to the list for her, which, come to think of it, wasn't such a great idea as now she'll know I was in her room and—

"Jamie, what do you want?"

Elin snaps her book shut and hides it away inside her jacket.

"Are you planning your birthday party?" I ask, sitting down beside her. She doesn't move over, so I end up hanging off the edge of the bench with the corner sticking into my bum. "What are you going to ask for? Riding lessons?"

"Why would you think that? Have you been in my room?" Elin's eyes narrow, and for a second I think laser beams are going to come shooting out of them.

Before my head can explode looking for an excuse, I catch

sight of a loose picture on the ground that must've slipped out of her book when she wasn't looking.

"Cos of this!" I snatch it up and wave it at her triumphantly. It's a drawing of Elin dressed as a princess riding a white horse, just like the one she's got on her bedside table.

Elin grabs the picture off me and stuffs it into her jacket. "Don't touch my things. Ever."

"So are you going to ask for a horse, or just riding lessons?" I try again. "A horse would be so cool. You could keep it in the back garden and Dad could build a shed for it. I'm going to get a remote-controlled helicopter for Christmas and then for my birthday I'm going to get—"

"You think money just grows on trees, don't you?" Elin snaps. She's got her creepy doll face on again, and her eyes are like little chips of ice. I can't tell what she's thinking, so I just have to guess.

"Uh-uh, but that would be awesome! Imagine if we planted a ten-pound note, and it grew into a big money tree, then we could—"

"Don't be so stupid!" Elin interrupts me before I can tell her my totally brilliant plan for spending all the cash we'd grow in the back garden next to the horse shed. "My mum can't even afford to get riding lessons for my birthday, never mind an actual horse."

"Why not?" I blink, confused. "I mean, Dad just bought me a TV and a new game console and a smartphone so I can video chat with Mum, and next weekend we're going shopping for a better microscope so I can be the best scientist ever!"

"Exactly! So where do you think the money my mum's been saving for my riding lessons has gone, hmm?"

Elin's glaring at me like she's expecting an answer. Before I can work it out, a girl from our class with messy hair and big glasses comes shuffling up to us. She looks even more scared of Elin than I do. She reaches into her jacket and pulls out a book that's a bit bent and stained and hands it over.

"Thanks for letting me read this," she says shyly. "I really liked it, especially the bit about—"

"I told you to give that back to me ages ago! It's overdue at the library now." Elin doesn't look happy to get her book back, she looks mad.

"Oh! I'm sorry, I got so into the story I wanted to finish it. Did you like the evil robot or the warrior princess best? I thought the robot was brilliant! It was so exciting when it—"

"I *told* you not to get this book messed up! Look what you've done to it! The cover's all bent, and what's that on the pages? Were you eating crisps when you read it?"

The girl's face goes all wobbly like jelly and she mumbles an apology and backs away. She's gone before I can tell her I've read the book too and the evil robot is the best thing ever. Maybe Elin doesn't like the robot because it reminds her too much of herself.

"It's a good book," I tell Elin instead, "but the second one's even better. Have you read it yet? There's this one bit where—"

"Why are you still here?"

Elin's scowling at me like I'm wearing my pyjamas in the middle of the playground.

"Er… just… nothing. I'm bored. Do you want to go and look for ants in the grass?"

"Jamie, I'm only going to say this once, so listen carefully." Elin takes a deep breath like talking to me is a huge effort. "Don't speak to me in school, OK? Don't even look at me. You're not my stepbrother, and you're definitely not my friend. Leave me alone, understand?"

I blink at her again, then I go and sit on the step by the senior years' door by myself.

I was wrong.

There are rules out here in the playground after all.

The rest of the morning is one long torture session of trying to stay in my seat and not shout out the answers to easy science questions or get ink stains on my brand new jotters when I scribble things out. At least the classroom assistant Miss Finlay is nice, and with her help I manage to make it to the lunch bell without getting yelled at again.

If class was bad though, it's nothing compared to lunch. I nearly go off my head when I open my lunchbox to find Elin's filled it with cheese sandwiches. She put them there to wind me up, I *know* she did. I've told her a million times the only sandwiches I like are jam or peanut butter. Cheese is a big block of smelly earwax and toenail fungus and bogies.

She's sitting on the other side of the dinner hall watching me right now, waiting for me to have another meltdown. I think she likes seeing me go crazy cos it makes her look so perfect in comparison. I don't get why we can't just be friends. Maybe if I give her my Transformers torch for her birthday she'll like me.

It's my best thing, but maybe if it's her best thing instead we can be friends.

I take a big deep breath prescribed by Doctor Mackay and push my cheese sandwiches away with the edge of my banana so I don't have to touch them. I'll throw them in the bin when the monitor's not looking.

"Hey! You have to eat those! You're not allowed to waste food."

Oh.

Great.

The one girl who hates me even more than Elin does is on lunch duty. Rachel's been laughing at me all morning with her nasty friend Lauren. She even told the teacher that I'd pushed her at break. I don't know what her problem is, I mean, I haven't even been here a whole day, so I haven't had time to do anything to annoy her yet, have I?

"I'm going to eat them," I tell Rachel, "I'm just having my banana first."

Rachel doesn't go away though. She just stands there waiting for me to eat my sandwiches. She must've guessed I can't stand them from the faces I was making.

"Come on Freak-Boy, get them eaten." Rachel grins at me, and her mean eyes go all small and beady.

Freak-Boy. I thought I'd escape that name when I moved here. Maybe I have it tattooed to my forehead or something and I'm the only one who can't see it.

"I *will* eat them, just give me a minute."

I'm getting anxious again. The thought of cramming those

slices of orange crud into my mouth and swallowing them is making my stomach churn.

"Your face is going all red Freak-Boy, do you fancy me or something? Or are you going to kick another tantrum? What are you, three years old?"

"Leave me alone," I snap, balling my fists to hold onto my temper. "Go away!"

"Not until you eat those sandwiches. Every. Last. Bit."

"I don't want to!" My hands are starting to shake. The Hulk is about to be unleashed.

All the kids at my dinner table are looking at me, and any minute now a teacher's going to come over and ask what the problem is. Then there'll be real fireworks.

"Fine. There's Miss Morrison. I'm going to tell her, and she'll *make* you eat them." Rachel marches off with a smug look on her face, and I start gasping for breath, trying to stay in control. I hate cheese sandwiches. I *hate* cheese sandwiches. I HATE CHEESE—

"Here," the girl sitting opposite says. "Swap?"

She pushes a couple of sandwiches wrapped in cling film across the table and picks up my cheese ones.

"What?" I was so ready for a big blow-up, it's like having all the air sucked out of me.

"Do you want to swap sandwiches? I don't mind cheese."

The girl blinks at me through huge glasses that make her look like a mouse with space telescopes attached to her eyes. I unwrap her sandwiches and examine them suspiciously. They're a bit squashed like they've been sitting at the bottom of her bag, but they're definitely, unmistakeably and without a doubt, raspberry jam.

I smile at the girl so hard my mouth hurts.

I think I've just found my new best friend.

Miss Morrison comes marching over to find me filling my face with sandwich and looking up at her all innocently and well behaved. She scowls, but I'm eating my lunch and she's got no reason to shout at me, so she goes to give Rachel a row for wasting her time instead.

Ha! I win!

"I'm Paige," the girl opposite says so quietly I almost don't hear her. "Paige Munro?" It sounds like a question. I don't know what the answer is.

Paige Munro is the one who gave Elin her book back in the playground at break. I don't know why Elin didn't want to talk to her. Paige Munro seems really nice.

"So…" I take a big bite of bread and jam and ask her the most important question in all the world. "Do you like the Transformers?"

19

Elin

"Elin! Jamie!" Mum called over the sound of Jamie's clattering in the kitchen. "It's family time. Come and play Monopoly."

"Just a minute!" I called back. I had just finished colouring in the drawing of my dream castle cake. I might not be able to get riding lessons for my birthday, but I was determined to plan my party and my cake to perfection.

I put my felt tips down and trudged into the kitchen. I didn't look forward to family time any more. At least when it was just me, Mum and Paul, we didn't spend the whole time arguing. The last few weeks had been a nightmare. It didn't matter how many sticker reward charts Mum put up on the wall, Jamie couldn't even brush his teeth or get himself out of bed in the morning without a fight. There weren't enough Transformers stickers in the whole universe to bribe the Monster into acting like a normal human being.

I stuck my birthday cake pictures on the fridge so Mum could see exactly how I wanted it to look, nearly getting hit on the head when Jamie opened the door yet again to reach in for even more jam and cream.

"Jamie! Use a plate, you're making a mess!" I cried, watching in horror as he slapped two slices of bread down on the counter and began slathering big slabs of peanut butter across them.

"I'm so hungreee!" he sang. "I could eat a horse. Oh, don't worry Elin, if you get one for your birthday I won't eat it, cross-my-heart-hope-to-die I won't."

"Maybe if you'd just eaten your dinner tonight instead of arguing with Mum about it you wouldn't be eating junk now," I muttered.

Our kitchen had become a battle zone where Jamie had a meltdown if he didn't get exactly what he wanted, when he wanted it. I was losing the war so badly he even had us eating dinner every night from his own specially selected menu of three meals. If I saw one more plate of sweet and sour chicken I was going to scream.

"I wasn't hungry then, but now I am," Jamie shrugged, scooping out half a jar of jam and piling it on top of the peanut butter mountain. "Hey! Do you want to try my Mad Jamie Specials?" he asked eagerly. "You haven't had one yet. They're the best thing ever. Dad totally loves them."

"Jamie, that's *enough*!" I snapped, wiping up the mess he was making with the whipped cream. "I'm so sick of cleaning up after you."

"Sorry," he mumbled through a mouthful of sandwich, dropping more on the floor.

I stomped into the living room to help Mum set the Monopoly board up, leaving Jamie to make a half-hearted attempt at mopping the cream up with his sleeve.

Mum and Paul both smiled at me while I set out the piles of bank notes and property cards, but both of them were faking. When Jamie came in covered in jam and cream and plonked himself down on the sofa, their smiles became even more strained. Paul glanced at Mum, scared she was going to blow up, but Mum frowned and held her tongue, trying to keep the peace.

It wouldn't take much for them to start yelling at each other. I hated arguments, but if I wanted rid of Jamie, I had to stir things up so they couldn't deny what a terrible idea it was for him to live with us.

I waited till Jamie had spent all of his money going round the board buying up everything in sight, then made sure I nudged the dice too close for him to be able to resist. He grabbed them and rolled straight away, his eyes lighting up when he saw where he'd landed.

"Jamie, it's not your turn!" I told him, moving his Monopoly piece back to where it was supposed to be and handing the dice to Mum.

"Hey! I rolled a seven!" Jamie yelled. "I'm going to buy Mayfair."

"No, you're not. It's Mum's go, you need to wait."

"But that's not fair!"

"Jamie, stop being such a stupid *baby*!"

"I'm not a baby! *Dad!* Tell her to—"

"ENOUGH!" Paul brought his hand down so hard on the table the board rattled. "This is supposed to be fun family time, not feeding time at the zoo! Could you two please try to get along for just five minutes?"

"But he's *cheating*!" I insisted.

"Elin, just drop it, OK? Look Jamie, here's Mayfair, that's four hundred you owe the bank." Paul tried to smooth things over, but his fake smile was no match for Jamie's real fury.

"I haven't got four hundred! I need the money Elin owes me for rent from the last round."

"I don't owe you any rent, you missed it! It's too late!"

I knew all of Jamie's triggers by now. I knew exactly what set him off, and I made sure I pressed those buttons as hard as I could.

"If you can't afford Mayfair then you'll have to buy it another time." I took the card off him and returned it to the bank. Then I sat back and waited for the fireworks display.

It took all of point five seconds for the rockets to go off.

"I HATE this game! It's STUPID!"

Jamie jumped up, overturned the whole board and raced out of the room.

Mum finally opened her mouth, but the words that came out weren't nice ones.

"That's it! I've tried everything from reward charts to time out, but nothing's working. Paul, he's got to go on medication, it's the only thing he hasn't tried yet."

"No way." Paul threw the Monopoly board back in its box and crumpled all the money as he snatched it up off the floor. "That's not happening. Jamie doesn't need to be drugged. He's not *sick*, Liz. There's nothing wrong with him that can't be fixed with a bit of—"

"Nothing *wrong* with him?" Mum looked like she was ready to explode. "He's got ADHD, Paul! It's not something you can just brush under the carpet. You can't keep ignoring—"

"Elin, go to your room," Paul interrupted, catching sight of me sitting there watching them argue.

"Why? What have I done wrong?" I cried, struggling to gulp back the growing anger before it could burst out. All the rage I'd been bottling up since Jamie arrived was bubbling up so fiercely inside me I felt like a volcano ready to erupt.

"Just do as you're told, Elin," Mum snapped.

"I *always* do as I'm told!" I protested, "and you just ignore me! Nobody asked if I wanted to share my house with that monster, you just moved him in! You never ask me what I want for dinner, or what I want to watch on TV or what I want to do at the weekend, you just ask Jamie! It's not fair! Maybe if I acted crazy like *him* you'd pay me more attention!"

Where did that *come from?*

The lava had erupted from my mouth before I could stop it, and I could feel the angry words scorching my throat on their way out.

"Elin, that's enough! Go to your room right now!" Paul shouted.

"You're not my dad! You can't tell me what to do!" I yelled back. My face was hot and my hands were balled up into fists, and before I knew it I was running to my room anyway to avoid crying in front of them.

I threw myself down on my bed and hid my face under my pillow. My whole body was shaking. I'd never felt so mad before, and it scared me. Was this how Jamie felt all of the time? No wonder he was always running away from people. I felt so ashamed at losing my temper I wanted to hide from the world.

What was happening to me? In the space of a few months I'd gone from the perfect daughter and student to a perfect mess. Jamie was ruining my reputation at school, and now he was making it look like all the arguing at home was my fault too.

"What am I going to do, Athena?" I sniffed, holding on to my painted horse and stroking her nose. "I wish things could go back to the way they were before."

For a moment, the little horse's eyes seemed to be looking over my shoulder. I turned round, and there, pinned to the wall beside family photos, were more drawings of my fairy-tale castle cake. Hanging on the door of my wardrobe was the beautiful sequinned top Gran had given me to go with my party jeans, and sitting on the shelf was a gorgeous handbag Dad had sent in the post this morning. I brushed a tear from my eye before it could fall and gave Athena a watery smile.

"My birthday on Saturday's going to fix a lot of things," I told her. "Everything will get better after that."

After my amazing party all the girls at school would like me and I'd have friends again like I used to. That would give me the courage to keep fighting the war.

All I had to do was be brave like the Perfect Princess in my story, and defeat the Monster. Mum would get sick of all the arguing and split up with Paul, and he and Jamie would have to leave. Once Paul was gone, Dad would come home to us. He'd start working again, and we'd have enough money to move back to Whitburn together. I'd get horse-riding lessons just like I was promised, and we'd live happily ever after, just like in my fairy tale.

I reached into my desk drawer, pulled out my story folder, and started writing.

The day of the party had arrived, and it was the most perfect birthday the kingdom had ever celebrated...

20

Jamie

I turn up the TV to drown out the sound of arguing and sit under the tent I've made from my quilt and chairs. Liz keeps dismantling it and making my bed, and I keep putting my tent right back up as soon as she's done. She says this is my home now, but how can it be if I'm not even allowed to have my room the way I want it? Under here in the dark, reading comics by the light of my Transformers torch, is the only place in the world where I feel safe.

"Stop yelling!" I plead, rocking back and forth as Dad and Liz shout at each other in the living room. "Please, just *stop*!"

Angry voices follow me everywhere I go, and even the noise of my own racing thoughts isn't loud enough to shut them up.

The smartphone Dad bought me pings from somewhere under a pile of school books, making me jump. I find it after a bit of rummaging, and I see I've missed a video call from Mum. I should ring her right back, but my finger hovers over the call button, and I can't make myself press it. She'll ask me how things are going, and even if I tell her everything's great, she'll just end up getting upset.

Mum always knows when I'm lying.

I scroll through the pictures she's sent, trying to ignore the stabbing pain right through my heart at the way she's smiling and the way Chris has his arms draped round her. I don't want Mum to be sad. It's been a long time since I've seen her looking so relaxed, and I know that's all my fault for being so difficult.

But the funny thing is, I don't want Mum to be happy either.

I don't want her having the time of her life in sunny California and forgetting all about me. I don't want Chris taking my place as the most important person in her life. I don't want to wake up every morning in a different house half a world away and eat my breakfast with a different woman who isn't Mum and who doesn't know how to cut my toast the way I like it, and who doesn't laugh when I tell her Mum's favourite jokes.

I don't think the universe cares very much about what I want, though.

"Jamie, turn that TV down!" Dad yells from the hall. I press the volume button quickly, hoping he'll come in for a chat and tell me everything's alright again, but he doesn't. I hear the front door slamming and the sound of his car engine, and I know things are really, really bad.

He used to go for long drives on his own before he split up with Mum. I think it was his way of avoiding arguments. I wish I could drive. Maybe if I went fast enough I'd be able to zoom away before I had my meltdowns, then Mum wouldn't have had to go all the way to America to avoid them.

It's getting hot under my tent. I crawl out and look for something to do that'll help me forget the game I spoiled and the shouting I caused. I flick through the TV channels, but there's nothing on. I can't be bothered reading, and I don't understand my homework, and Liz has confiscated my games console cos I got too many sad faces on my behaviour chart, and…

I'm bored.

I wish Dad would let me take medicine for my ADHD. It would be nice to have an ordinary brain that wasn't always fluttering off when I needed to use it. Maybe when I grow up and I'm a mad scientist I'll be able to make my own cure for ADHD.

Hey! That's a great idea.

I grab my chemistry set and get to work, mixing up a whole load of chemicals in test tubes and trying to make something that won't taste like decomposing skunk. I figure if my brain is fizzing like cola and mints then I need something that's going to neutralise it. I know all about acids and alkalis, and last year I worked my way through a big book full of experiments to test how different chemicals react with each other.

I know how to fill a balloon full of carbon dioxide by mixing lemon juice and baking soda in a bottle.

I know how to make water glow in the dark by soaking a highlighter pen in it and shining an ultraviolet lamp through it.

I know how to make a lava lamp with vegetable oil and water and fizzy aspirin tables that make the oil bob up and down.

The only thing I don't know is what'll happen when I drink the strange brown liquid I'm measuring out into a beaker.

A few seconds later I find out, and it takes nearly a whole roll of toilet paper to clean the sick off my best trainers.

OK, no more experiments till my stomach stops bubbling like a witch's cauldron.

I leave my science kit spread out all over my table and go and sit on my bed, flicking through the TV channels again and feeling like a failure. I wish I could do something right, something *good* for once. I wish I could prove I'm not always a selfish monster who makes everyone upset. I've already wrapped up my Transformers torch to give to Elin for her birthday, but I don't think that's going to be enough to stop her hating me.

Then I have a genius idea.

I know exactly how to make someone else happy for once! I can't make Elin happy cos all her riding-lesson money's been blown on my stuff, and Mum's far off in California, and I've no idea how to fix Dad or Liz and make them stop yelling at each other. But there's someone else who deserves to have something nice happen to them.

I tiptoe into the kitchen like I'm James Bond on a mission. I find what I'm looking for inside the stationery drawer, and carry one of the precious cards back to my room.

It takes me ages to fill it out, and I get some chemical stains on the envelope, but I've used my best handwriting so most of the words are on the line and they aren't all running into each other for once.

I grin as I slide the card into the damp envelope and put it in my schoolbag for tomorrow.

Elin's having the best birthday party in the world on Saturday, and I'm going to make sure the nicest person in the world will be there.

21

Elin

"What are you doing here?"

When I opened the front door the last person in the world I wanted to see was standing on my doorstep.

"Happy Birthday, Elin," Paige Munro said nervously, handing over a small box wrapped in paper so crumpled it looked like it had been recycled about five times.

I held it at arm's length and stared at her. Why was she here? I didn't invite her. What on earth made her think she could just turn up like this?

Despite her huge glasses, Paige wasn't blind. She could read my reluctance to let her in written in big letters across my face.

"I got an invitation for the party. Look!" She held up one of my special balloon-shaped cards. The handwriting on it wasn't mine. There was only one person in the universe who wrote that messily. The ink was stained and the card had dark patches where something brown and stinky had been spilled on it.

It smelled exactly like Jamie's room.

That little freak!

How DARE he try to ruin my party by inviting people without my permission! It was bad enough I'd had to invite Rachel and Lauren, but now I'd have to take Paige Munro to the Adventure Dome too?

NO WAY!

Mum was at the door before I could slam it in Paige's face.

"Oh! Did you invite someone else, Elin? I thought just twelve girls were coming. You're Paige, aren't you? Come on in, you're just in time."

I left Paige hovering anxiously in the hall and followed Mum into the kitchen. My head was buzzing with anger. This was supposed to be my special day, and Jamie was ruining it already. If he hadn't been under strict instructions to stay in his room until the minibus left, I'd have flattened him.

"I didn't invite Paige, Mum!" I protested, careful to keep my voice down so the big group of girls giggling in the living room wouldn't hear me. "It was Jamie! He stole one of my invitation cards and—"

"Don't make a fuss about it now Elin, there's a spare seat on the minibus, so it's not a problem."

Mum was multi-tasking like she was at work, packing snacks into bags and checking there were enough cans of cola to go round. She didn't have the time or the energy to listen to me complaining.

She hadn't had time for me at all since the Monster came to live with us.

"That's the driver with the minibus now," Mum said, hearing the roar of the engine outside. "Go and tell the girls it's time to go.

And for goodness' sake Elin, try not to look so miserable! It's supposed to be a party."

Yeah, it was supposed to be *my* party, with the people *I* invited.

I stomped past Paige in the hall and went into the living room to tell everyone to grab their coats. The girls were buzzing with excitement at the thought of going to the Adventure Dome. It was the most amazing place in Glasgow, and the most expensive. Gran always said you couldn't buy friends, but I was hoping she was wrong. Jamie and his new gadgets might have stopped me getting the horse-riding lessons I'd been dreaming of, but thanks to Mum and Dad my party would make me the most popular girl in my class.

It wasn't Mum and Dad who paid for the cake and the Adventure Dome though, a little voice whispered at the back of my head.

Yes it was! I hissed back. *Shut up!* I wasn't about to admit where the money really came from. I didn't want to have to be grateful to the Wicked Witch for anything.

"Are you coming?" I called. Rachel and Lauren were giggling together in the corner. I was pretty sure it was me they were talking about.

"Yeah. Nice top Elin, by the way," Rachel said as she pulled on her jacket. "I didn't know Oxfam sold party clothes."

I gritted my teeth and pretended I didn't hear her.

Their giggles got louder when they saw Paige hanging about in the hallway.

"Aw, that's nice, you've invited your best friend!" Lauren laughed. "Is your boyfriend coming too or has he been locked in his padded cell for the day?"

"Jamie's not her boyfriend, he's her *brother*," Rachel grinned. "Isn't he, Elin?"

I took a deep breath and tried to keep the polite smile pasted on my face. "Jamie's not coming to the Adventure Dome. Girls only. He's helping his dad get the party food ready for us coming back."

That was why there was a spare seat on the minibus. There was no way I was letting Jamie embarrass me and ruin my special day, even though he'd been desperate to come. His meltdown when I told him he wasn't welcome had been spectacular. I guess inviting Paige was his idea of revenge.

I looked back before I closed the front door. Jamie was standing at the far end of the hall outside his room, watching us leave. He was clutching one of my 'Happy 12th Birthday' balloons and an advertising leaflet for the Adventure Dome. He looked like a sad clown who'd been left behind by the circus.

I hesitated on the doorstep, suddenly feeling like the worst person in the whole world. Jamie had been looking forward to my party almost as much as I had. He hadn't shut up about it for weeks.

I glanced over at the hall table where the Transformers torch he'd given me lay on a pile of wrapping paper. It was his favourite thing, and he'd gone and given it to me for my birthday even though I didn't want it. He'd put in a new set of batteries and even stuck some glitter stars on it so it would match my favourite T-shirt. He was trying so hard to be my friend it almost hurt to see him look so disappointed.

Maybe Paul could bring him to the Adventure Dome in the car and he could just run about in one of the other play areas, I thought.

If Paul was there to watch then maybe it wouldn't be so bad if I let him come and—

"What's the hold-up, Elin?" Rachel called over. "Are you missing your weirdo brother already?"

There was a chorus of giggles from the girls boarding the minibus, and I felt my face burn with embarrassment. The Monster was spoiling my perfect party already and he wasn't even coming.

I slammed the door shut and pretended I hadn't seen him.

Jamie

I want to go to the Adventure Dome more than anything.

The leaflet says there's an intergalactic space ride where you go on this giant rocket that's so real you think you're going to another planet, and a jungle room where there are snakes and giant lizards you can hold. I bet Elin won't be interested in any of that. She'll just want to play in the stupid fairy castle with the other girls in our class.

What's the point of going to the Adventure Dome if you don't do all the best things?

I bet Paige would like the space ride and the jungle room. We spent all lunchtime yesterday hunting for ladybirds in the grass by the football pitch. We didn't catch any since it's nearly winter, but Paige found the broken shell of a magpie's egg, and I found a spider with legs the length of my little finger. She knows almost as much about insects as I do, and she likes the same nature programmes on the BBC. She doesn't watch the Discovery Channel though. Her mum can't afford to pay for satellite TV.

I wish Paige was my stepsister instead of Elin. I bet she would have been dead excited to get my Transformers torch, instead of making a face like she was sucking lemons when she unwrapped it.

I drum my fingers against the wall and count to twenty as I listen to the minibus reversing out of the drive, waiting till it turns onto the main road. Dad and Liz said I have to stay out of the kitchen until the girls have gone, but I think that was more Liz's idea than Dad's. He wasn't happy that Elin wouldn't let me go with them, but I don't think he can take any more arguing with Liz.

It's like we're all walking on magpie's eggshells round each other now, trying not to break anything. It was like this at home before Dad left, and I'm scared if I do anything to upset him and Liz then Dad will leave again, and what'll happen to me after that? Mum doesn't want me in California, and Liz and Elin definitely don't want me here. Where would I go?

Maybe I could move in with Paige and her mum. I think Paige would like that. She doesn't have any brothers or sisters or a dad, and she seems pretty lonely.

I hope she has fun today. I hope Rachel and Lauren aren't mean to her when I'm not there to stick up for her. And I hope Elin isn't going to make her feel bad for having a fake invitation instead of a real one. Especially as I didn't tell Paige it was me who wrote it.

"Jamie? Are you going to give me a hand in here?"

Dad's in the kitchen getting the party food ready, and he's letting me know the coast is clear and I can come out. I run down the hall and charge into the kitchen at top speed, tripping over a chair and knocking over some of the cups Dad is laying out on the table.

"Careful! Elin will have a fit if you wreck her cake," Dad warns, checking to make sure I haven't dented the pink icing. It's the biggest cake I've ever seen, a triple-decker sponge cake in the shape of a giant fairy castle with turrets. It's got so many sweets on it I'm pretty sure one bite would rot all your teeth. After Elin refusing to let me go to the Adventure Dome, I grin at the thought of her spending tomorrow at the dentist getting her teeth pulled out one by one. Then I remember that Paige will be eating the cake too when they come back, and suddenly it doesn't seem as funny any more.

"No, not sandwiches Jamie, we talked about that." Dad closes the fridge door before I can start pulling out the jam jars and cans of cream I've stashed there.

"But my Mad Jamie Specials are the best thing ever!" I protest. "Everyone will love them."

"We've already got enough food to feed an army," Dad says, pointing at the piles of buns and bowls of trifle and sweets. He's got a point, but I don't want to admit it.

"Not even a few? I can just do one each."

"Not today Sandwich Man, you know Elin doesn't like them."

"She's never even tried them," I mutter, picking up the extra one wrapped in cling film I'd left on the kitchen counter for her. It was a special birthday one, and she'd just pushed it away and said, "Yuck!" when I'd offered it to her this morning.

"And put that one away in the fridge. You can blow up these balloons instead." Dad hands me the pump. "I need to finish setting the table."

The cardboard tube's a bit rubbish, and no matter how hard I pump there's only a tiny little puff of air coming out the end. I'd much rather use lemon juice and baking soda to blow up the balloons, but I don't think Dad would let me do one of my science experiments just now. He's looking a bit stressed. I think he's worried about what's going to happen when all the girls come back and I join them for the party food. He doesn't need to worry. I'm going to be on my very best behaviour.

I'm only one meltdown short of being kicked out of this family for good.

I can't afford to do anything wrong ever again.

23

Elin

"That was the best birthday trip EVER!" Rachel grinned at me across the table and stuffed another bun in her mouth, and I grinned back.

"Yeah, awesome party Elin, thanks for inviting us." This time Lauren wasn't being sarcastic. For once she actually meant it. They stopped laughing at me when we got to the giant castle at the Adventure Dome, and we had an amazing time exploring the creepy dungeons and having a pretend battle in plastic armour in the tournament ring. Rachel even helped me put on make-up in the dressing-up room, and Lauren took loads of selfies of the three of us together to post online.

The party was going brilliantly, and everyone was fussing round me like I was a real princess. For the first time since I came to Glasgow, I actually had friends.

All I needed was a few more pieces of my plan to fall into place, and my fairy-tale ending would come true at last.

Even having Paige here was turning out to be less awful than I expected. I ignored her the whole time we were at the Adventure

Dome, but when we got back home for food she sat with Jamie at the far end of the table and babbled away with him like we were in the school canteen. At least she was keeping him from annoying the other girls. It was funny – she never said more than three words to anyone else in school, but she couldn't seem to shut up around Jamie.

"Time to cut the cake, Elin," Mum said, lighting the twelve big candles. She was still looking a bit flustered. I was pretty sure she'd be glad when this was all over and the thirteen girls crammed round our kitchen table went home.

"Make a wish! Oh no, wait! Just a second, I need to find my phone so I can take a picture." Mum went rummaging in her handbag and then her coat pocket, but she couldn't find it.

"It's alright, I'll take the pictures with mine." Paul held his up, but Mum shook her head.

"I have to find my phone, I need it for work. Can you give it a ring so I can hear where I've put it?"

Paul called Mum's phone, but there wasn't an answering ring from anywhere in the kitchen. "Maybe you left it in the minibus? I could give the company a call to check? If it's not there then I'll try the Adventure Dome."

Paul disappeared into the living room to make some calls, and Mum rummaged in her handbag again, looking more and more worried.

"Can I blow the candles out now?" I asked. "Everyone wants cake." I didn't want my beautiful castle cut up into little bits, but I didn't want Rachel and Lauren sticking their spoons in and digging chunks out of the wall either. They looked like they were getting ready to pull the whole thing to pieces if Mum didn't hurry up.

"Just a minute, I need to find my phone first." Mum went out to see if Paul was having any luck, and when I turned round I found Rachel and Lauren leaning over the table, playing with the candles on my cake.

"Bet you can't do this," Rachel dared the other girls, passing her fingers through the flames. Before I could stop them all the girls were trying it, giggling as they swiped their fingers over the candles at top speed and nearly knocking the castle towers down.

"Hey! Be careful!" I warned. I didn't want my cake ruined before Mum got a chance to take some pictures of it.

"Don't be such a boring swot, Elin," Rachel muttered. "It's just a bit of fun."

I watched her burn the end of a streamer in the flame without saying anything, hoping I hadn't spoiled my chances of being popular. Rachel dropped the burning paper onto a plate, and Lauren grabbed a plastic fork and started melting the end in the flames, trying to get the whole thing to disappear in a little ball of hot goo.

"Hey! This is just like one of my science experiments!" Jamie said, jumping up to grab one of the burst balloons he'd blown up way too full and holding it above the candles. The smell of burning rubber filled the kitchen, and it went on smouldering after he dropped it onto the plate and blew on his singed fingers.

"Look, Freak-Boy's starting a bonfire!" Rachel grinned, adding a couple of streamers and another plastic fork to the burning heap on the plate. Everyone held their noses and watched the small flames turn blue and green as the plastic and rubber burned.

"Why's it going a funny colour?" Paige asked. "I thought fire was supposed to be red and orange."

"Different chemicals turn flames different colours," Jamie said like he was a professor giving a lecture. "Look at this." He grabbed one of my glittery birthday cards off the shelf and threw it onto the plate before I could stop him. The glitter crackled and the flames changed colour again, but I was so mad at Jamie I didn't care how pretty it looked.

"That was my card!" I yelled. "Stop it Jamie, you're going to set the smoke alarm off."

But Jamie had an audience for his science experiments, and he wasn't listening any more. He went running to the cupboard under the sink, and took out the bottle of turpentine I used to clean the paint off my brushes.

"This is a great experiment!" he told everyone. "You wouldn't think liquid burns, would you? But it does, just watch this!"

There was a horrible moment where I knew exactly what was going to happen, but I couldn't get round the table fast enough to snatch the bottle off Jamie before he could unscrew the lid and tip it up over the plate.

I think he only meant to pour out a few drops, but he was so full of sugar and fizzy cola his hands were shaking. Instead a whole torrent of turpentine came flooding from the bottle, splashing over the plate, across the table and onto the floor.

There was a strange whooshing sound, and in an instant my entire birthday party came to a blazing end in an eruption of flames.

24

Jamie

The firefighters have just left.

They tried to talk to me, but I was crying so hard I couldn't hear anything they were saying.

Everyone's gone home. There were a lot of shouting parents and frightened girls sobbing outside, but it's all quiet now. Liz is in Elin's room trying to calm her down, and Dad's in the kitchen throwing all the bits of burnt table into the back garden. The whole house smells like charcoal. It's making me feel like throwing up, but I don't want to climb out from under my quilt where I'm hiding.

I can't believe I did something so *stupid*.

I've done a lot of crazy things, but even for me that was spectacularly dumb.

What the hell is wrong with my brain? Why can't I just think like normal people instead of doing the first mad thing that comes into my head?

I made Paige cry, and that hurts even more than making Elin cry.

Paige will forgive me for scaring her though, I know she will. Elin won't ever forget that I ruined her birthday party. Her giant castle cake went up in a blaze of flames, and she didn't even get any pictures of it before I spoiled it. She's going to want revenge when she calms down. Maybe I should just let her build a big bonfire out of all my best things. Maybe that would be enough to stop her hating me.

The thought of seeing more flames makes my shaking worse, and before I know it I'm crying again. It doesn't matter what I give Elin as payment for wrecking her birthday. Even if she forgives me, I'm never going to be able to stop hating myself.

"Jamie, can I come in for a minute?"

Dad's knocking at the door, but I don't get up. He comes in anyway and sits down on the end of my bed. "That was a pretty crazy day, eh Sandwich Man?" he sighs, giving my leg a shake. He doesn't sound angry or disappointed, he just sounds tired.

"I've been thinking… I don't like the idea of you taking medication for your ADHD, but we're kind of running out of options here, aren't we?"

There's a big pause, and when I just sniff instead of answering he says, "So what do you think, Jamie? Do you want to go back to the doctor with me and see what they say? Do you want to try taking something just for a little while to see if it'll help?"

"Will it make me normal?" I ask, throwing off the quilt and looking hopefully at Dad.

"I don't know son, I don't know what it'll do," Dad says, shaking his head. For the first time ever he doesn't correct me and tell me I'm fine just the way I am. He looks beaten, like a boxer who's taken too many punches. He's taken them for me all my life. It's my turn to do something for him. Something that will make him proud of me instead of always having to make excuses for my behaviour.

"OK Dad," I nod. "I'll take the medicine."

Part Three

Breaking Out

25

Elin

"And how are things back home, pet? Has everything settled down a bit?"

I knew what Dad was asking. He wanted to know if Jamie's ADHD medication was making him act like a normal human being after he nearly set the whole house on fire before Christmas.

"Sort of," I shrugged, picking the raisins off my snowman bun and putting them on Dad's plate. I knew all of his favourite things better than his fake family ever would. "Jamie's quieter now, at least."

'Quieter' wasn't even close to the truth. Jamie was a zombie since he'd started taking the medication. He hardly said a word to anyone, and he stayed in his room most of the time. At school he spent all day staring out the window. He didn't even do his science work any more, which was kind of weird, as he was the best in the class at experiments when he concentrated.

I bit my lip hard to make sure I didn't say that last thought out loud. I didn't want to admit to Dad that anyone could be better than me at anything, especially not Jamie.

"But he's behaving himself?" Dad frowned. "No more tantrums and dangerous antics?"

"Yeah, no more craziness," I said without enthusiasm. No matter how quiet he was round the house now, I'd never forgive him for ruining my birthday. But that wasn't the only thing he'd spoiled. Mum and Dad had a big argument when he found out what Jamie had done at my party, and they still weren't speaking. Instead of the happy Boxing Day at Gran's I'd been looking forward to, I was sitting on the sofa with Dad while Mum helped Gran make a fruit cake for New Year's Eve in the kitchen. This was the one time of year I got to spend with both Mum and Dad, and they didn't even want to be in the same room together.

The Monster had turned into the Ghost, but he was still haunting us.

"And how's school been going? Have you made some new friends this year?" Dad asked hopefully.

I shook my head. "Everyone makes fun of me all the time because of Jamie! My wrecked birthday party was all anyone talked about for weeks, and Rachel and Lauren won't shut up about it. They keep passing me drawings of my hair on fire and my cake turning into a pile of melted goo. I got mad at them last week and shouted at them, and Miss Morrison gave me extra homework for the first time ever, and—"

I shut my mouth quickly, wishing I hadn't opened it in the first place. Dad was never going to believe I was perfect now. Jamie had ruined that too.

"Don't worry, pet." Dad gave me a hug when he saw my bottom

lip wobble. "I'll talk to your mum about it."

"It won't help! Mum always takes his side, and Paul just tells me off when I complain about Jamie."

I was dangerously close to tears. I'd need to change the subject fast or I'd start crying and Dad would be really disappointed. I'd *promised* him when he left that I'd be brave and not cry. I couldn't let him down now.

"Paul tells you off?" I could see Dad's eyes narrow like he was about to get angry himself. I didn't want to talk about the Imposter and his stupid son for one more minute, and I definitely didn't want Dad marching into the kitchen to have another argument with Mum.

"There was one nice thing that happened in school though," I said quickly. "Our teacher says there's going to be a Junior Science Fair at the Science Centre in May, and all the schools in Glasgow are going to put forward their best entries for it. The prize for the winner is a thousand pounds!"

"Wow, that's some prize!" Dad whistled. "You could buy me a real Ferrari for that!" He picked up the model I'd spent weeks painting for his Christmas present and zoomed it around in the air making engine noises. He used to dream of having a really fancy car, but since he got divorced and left work to look after the Mutant, he couldn't afford to drive anything that wasn't second-hand.

His fake family had ruined everything for him too.

"I'm going to do a butterfly display," I told him. "I'll paint all of the wings and write about the different types and where they live, and it'll be the best entry ever!"

"That sounds brilliant," Dad grinned. "And what would you spend the thousand pounds on if you won?"

"Riding lessons, of course. The ones I was supposed to get for my birthday, except I couldn't because Mum and Paul spent all the money on Jamie's new stuff. The ones I couldn't get for Christmas because Jamie burned down the kitchen and we had to get everything replaced."

The ones I would've had long before now if you were working instead of staying at home all day looking after the Mutant, the mean little voice at the back of my head nearly made me say out loud.

Dad must've been able to read my mind, as his smile slipped a bit and he put the car back down with a sigh. "I know it's been hard for you, Elin. I'm going back to work in a few months. We'll get you those riding lessons soon, I promise."

"I know you will. You're the best dad in the world."

"And you're my Perfect Princess." He grabbed me round the waist and tickled my arm, and before I knew it I was in fits of giggles, play fighting with him just like I used to.

"Let go, you troll, or I'll run you through with my sword!"

"Never!" Dad grinned. "It's a fight to the death!" He found my weak spot just under my chin and tickled me till I was helpless with laughter. We were just grabbing cushions for a pillow fight when Mum put her head round the living-room door, her grim expression spoiling our fun.

"Get your coat Elin, we have to leave early."

"*What?* But Mum, we can't go now! It's hours till Dad has to drive back!"

"I'm sorry Elin, but Paul's had his shift changed at the last

144

minute and I need to get back to look after Jamie."

"That's not very fair on Elin, Liz." Dad was on his feet, scowling at Mum like this was all her fault. "I don't get to see her very often, and now we have to give up our Boxing Day together because of Paul and his son?"

"If you're too busy to come to Glasgow to see your own daughter then don't complain to me that you don't get to spend enough time with her!" Mum snapped.

Mum and Dad were arguing again like they used to, and it was all Jamie's fault.

"Stop it! That's quite enough, you two." Gran marched in and told them off like she was Miss Morrison and they hadn't done their homework. "This is supposed to be Boxing Day, not a boxing match! You're upsetting poor Elin."

"Sorry pet." Dad gave me a hug while Mum stomped off to get our coats. "I just miss you, that's all."

"I miss you too, Dad." I squeezed him back tightly.

"Time to go, Elin." Mum handed me my coat and hurried me to the car.

I waved at Dad and Gran through the window as we turned the corner, gazing back at Gran's Enchanted Cottage where nothing was ever supposed to change. It had today though. Mum and Dad hadn't argued like that in years. Jamie had managed to ruin our family reunion without even being there.

I was doing my best to put my real family back together again, but there was a big Jamie-shaped wall keeping us apart.

I was going to knock it down and get Dad back, even if I had to take Jamie apart piece by piece to do it.

Jamie

The house still smells funny, like a damp bonfire.

We put up a real Christmas tree, and Liz has been spraying pine air freshener everywhere for weeks, but it hasn't helped.

Everything still stinks of Eau de Jamie-Went-and-Burned-the-House-Down.

It's late. I'm tired, but I can't get to sleep.

I take my Transformers torch from my bedside table and switch it on. Elin doesn't want it. She threw it back at me when I ruined her birthday party.

I open the book Paige gave me for Christmas and try to read it. It's a book about butterflies.

I know it is, cos there's a big picture of a butterfly on the cover.

I can't seem to focus on the words though.

I'm *so* tired.

My head is all mushy like it's full of candy floss that someone's dropped in a puddle.

I stretch out on my bed and flick through the photographs

in the book slowly, letting my eyes go all unfocused like I'm about to fall asleep.

I can't sleep though. Every night I lie awake and stare at the ceiling, waiting till it's time to get up again.

My brain won't switch off, but it won't switch on properly either.

It's like I'm a caterpillar that's got stuck inside its chrysalis and can't turn into a butterfly. My brain's racing, telling me I have to break out, but my body's tangled up in invisible threads.

It's like a bad dream, but I'm wide awake.

I can hear the sound of a bedroom door slamming, and the house goes quiet again.

Dad and Liz have finally stopped arguing.

They started as soon as Dad got home from his shift tonight.

Dad's upset because I'm not me any more, and Liz is upset because of something that happened at Elin's gran's house, but they're both taking it out on each other.

I thought taking the medication would solve everything, but all it's done is give Dad something else to worry about.

I'm not worried.

I'm too tired and too spaced out to feel much of anything at all.

The sound of footsteps in the hall stops outside my door. Dad must've seen the light from my Transformers torch.

"Are you awake, Jamie?"

He puts his head round the door, then when he sees me sitting up he comes in and switches on my bedside lamp.

"Still can't sleep, huh?" He says something else, but by the time I peel my eyes slowly off the book and look up I've forgotten what it is, and he has to repeat it.

"Is it a good book?" Dad asks again.

"Yeah," I shrug. It probably is. Paige gave it to me on the last day of term. It was wrapped in newspaper instead of Christmas paper, and the first page was torn out, so I think she stole it from the library and didn't want me to see the label. But it's the thought that counts.

I didn't think to get her anything.

I can't think of anything much at all any more.

Dad sits down on my bed, and I put my feet in his lap to keep them warm.

"Miss Morrison says your behaviour's got much better in class," Dad says, giving my feet a rub. My feet are the only bit of me I don't mind being touched. They used to be tickly and it always made me laugh.

Tonight I hardly feel it.

Dad waits for me to say something back, but when I don't he says, "She thinks you're finally starting to settle in, but you're not getting much work done. That's why you're getting so much homework even though you're behaving better. Is everything OK, Jamie?"

Maybe Dad's the one who needs medication. He's getting forgetful. We've had this conversation three times already since he went to see Miss Morrison at the end of term.

"It's fine," I say. It's not true, but it's what Dad wants to hear, so I say it anyway.

"Are you feeling OK? You've been a bit… quiet since you started the medication."

"I'm fine," I lie again.

"You'd tell me if there was anything wrong though, wouldn't you? You can stop taking the medication any time you want, you know that, right?"

"Yeah."

I don't have the energy to tell him the truth.

"Well, your teacher thinks if you could just concentrate a little more, you've got a great shot at winning a place at the science fair in May, isn't that great?"

Dad picks up the school leaflet from the floor where I dropped it and tries to get me excited about it.

I know I should care. Science is my best thing. There's a one-thousand-pound prize and everything.

I wish I could feel *something*.

I try to smile at Dad, but it comes out more like a shrug.

"It's late, you should get some sleep. We'll talk about it tomorrow, OK?" Dad frowns, but I'm not sure if he's worried or disappointed.

"Goodnight son." Dad tucks me back into bed and turns off the light again.

When I hear him in the bathroom, I turn my Transformers torch back on and pull Mum's Christmas card out from under my pillow.

There's lots of photos tucked inside, and I go through them slowly, putting the ones of Mum on her own on top of my quilt and dropping the ones that have Chris in them on the floor.

Mum's written messages on the back of them, but my mind's too fuzzy to read them right now. I know what they say though.

Mum says she loves me and she misses me and she hopes I have a wonderful Christmas with Dad in Scotland.

The one thing she doesn't say is 'I wish you were here'.

That's what people are supposed to say on messages from abroad.

Unless of course they actually like living on a different continent and they're glad to get away from you.

I put the photos of Mum inside the book Paige gave me for Christmas and slide it back under my pillow.

There's a big lump there now, but it doesn't matter.

I'm not going to sleep much tonight anyway.

I should probably stop taking the medication, but what's the point? Everything would just go back to the way it was before.

Except now instead of being a monster who stomps and roars and makes everyone unhappy, I'm almost invisible.

Maybe if I keep taking the medication then one day soon I'll disappear completely.

I'm pretty sure that's exactly what Elin wanted for Christmas.

27

Elin

It had been five whole months since Jamie turned up on our doorstep and I still hadn't managed to get rid of him.

What was worse, after New Year Paul took him back to the doctor and they tried a series of lower medication doses. After a few weeks he came back to life and stopped being the Ghost, but he didn't go back to being the Monster either. I didn't know what to call him any more.

Paul was calling him a 'trooper' and Mum kept saying he was 'really brave for trying so hard'. Even Miss Morrison had been praising his hard work. But I liked this new Jamie Lee even less than the old one. He beat me in the class maths quiz last week, and I was just about ready to strangle him.

It wasn't like the medication fixed him exactly – he still had meltdowns over stupid things like football practice being cancelled or finding out I put cheese sticks in his lunchbox. But it was as if he'd slowed down to a speed where he actually had time to *think* before he did things. He was still disorganised and messy and needed Mum to remind him to do his homework, but he actually got all of his science report done the other day and handed it in on time. Miss Morrison even told him this morning that he should put an entry in for the science fair.

Jamie was really good at science. His entry might even beat mine.

It was an awful thought. I had to get chosen to represent our school at the fair in May so I had a shot at winning. That would make Dad proud of me and show him how perfect I could be. Plus I needed that money for the riding lessons I'd been dreaming of. I *had* to win.

Jamie would just spend the money on a million packs of chewing gum and the world's biggest collection of Transformers stickers. I had to make sure he didn't win. I had to find a way to stop him.

I turned over the pages of my folder, filled with story after story of the Monster being defeated by the Perfect Princess. If only it was as easy to get rid of Jamie in real life.

It was a freezing-cold February, and sitting on the bench trying to write my story at break time with my thick gloves on wasn't easy. There wasn't anything else to do though – the Monster had ruined my chances of making any friends. Rachel the Troll, Lauren her shadow, and a big group of girls were hanging about by the senior entrance steps talking about starting high school in the autumn. Over on the basketball court some of the sporty girls were playing netball, and there were smaller groups standing around chatting and playing on their phones.

The only other girl on her own in the whole playground was Paige Munro, and there was no way I was desperate enough to start up a conversation with her.

I grinned as I read over the last story I'd written. The Princess had turned the Slug and the Monster into statues. She stuck them on posts on either side of the palace gates as a warning to the Troll and her goblin army that they were next.

The Slug might as well be a statue the way she's always staring at the Monster, I thought. Paige was standing at the side of the pitch, watching Jamie play football with the other boys who'd made the team. They weren't happy when he got picked, but they were alright about it after Jamie proved he could actually play. He still got mad when someone broke the rules, but as long as there was a referee and everyone played fair, he was just as good at scoring goals as Steven, the captain.

Steven had forgiven Jamie for stealing his football and let him hang about with his gang now. They'd even started texting Jamie after school, and last weekend Jamie went round to Darren's house to play computer games with them. Mum made sure he took his medication a bit later so it wouldn't wear off so soon, but it wasn't like it was a magic potion that actually turned Jamie into a normal human being or anything.

He was driving me crazy. Everyone kept making excuses for him and forgiving him when he blew up, but there was no way I could forgive him for wrecking my chances of getting riding lessons and ruining my birthday party. The last straw came when Miss Morrison moved him to my table today. I couldn't even escape him in class now. I clutched my pen harder as I wrote down all the bad things that could happen to the Monster in my story, wishing all the anger inside me didn't make my stomach ache so much.

I'd been *so* close to getting rid of him before Christmas, before the medication started working. With all the arguments he caused, Mum and Paul had almost split up. If Jamie had been unmanageable for just a *little* bit longer then Mum would've thrown Paul out and Jamie would've had to go with him. There had to be some way for me to turn him back into the Monster, there just had to.

"Hey Elin, you want to come and hunt for treasure with us?"

I stuffed my story folder into my bag quickly before scowling up at Jamie. He'd seen Paige standing on her own and had given up his game of football to play with her instead. Now they were crowding round my bench, holding up Jamie's spy kit magnifying glasses like they were a couple of junior detectives.

"Grow up and leave me alone," I sighed. "I'm busy."

Paige's face fell, but Jamie never knew when to quit.

"Aw, come on Elin, it'll be fun! Yesterday we found the ring that Miss Finlay lost, and today we're going to see what we can find in the grass by the car park. I've got a spare magnifying glass. Or you can have my best one if you like."

It was hard to keep scowling at them when I wanted more than anything to have people to talk to. I was good at finding things too. I always knew where to look for Mum's car keys, and I found the brooch that Gran lost the other week out in the garden. Jamie was right, it did sound like fun, better than freezing to death on the bench anyway.

The car park was round the side of the school. Maybe no one would notice me talking to Jamie and Paige back there? Maybe if I just spent one break time with them no one would think we were friends, or—

"Hey, look at the state of those two!" I heard Rachel call, and my heart sank down to the tips of my numb toes. "What are you, Sherlock Freak and his sidekick? Are you going to play detective with your brother and his girlfriend, Elin? Are you in their secret gang now?"

There was a loud snort of laughter from the other girls sitting on the step. There was no way I could hang around with Jamie and Paige now without getting laughed at too. There was only one way out of this.

"Shove your magnifying glass up your bum, Jamie Lee, and don't come near me again!" I snapped at him, loud enough for the girls on the steps to hear. "That goes for you too, Paige Munro. I'm not your friend and I never will be, OK?"

Paige looked like she was going to cry. Jamie just shrugged and put his spare magnifying glass back in his pocket like it was my loss and not his, and started to walk away.

He didn't get far.

Rachel wasn't going to let him go without getting a reaction out of him. She didn't like the fact that he'd found some friends and was fitting in better now.

"Hey, Freak-Boy!" Rachel hissed, digging her fingers into Jamie's arm and making him jump. "You set anyone else's kitchen on fire lately?"

Jamie tried to ignore her and keep walking, which wasn't like the old Jamie at all, but Rachel wouldn't let him go.

"Hey! I heard you made the football team – what did you do,

threaten to burn down the gym teacher's house if he didn't let you play?"

That made Lauren laugh, and the other girls all joined in. Jamie could handle people making fun of him, but he hated being touched by strangers. I could see it was taking every ounce of concentration for him not to blow up.

"Stop it, Rachel!" Paige said bravely. "Leave him alone." Her eyes were wide and scared, but she stood up for Jamie anyway, even though she knew she'd end up being the target.

"Can't you talk any more, Freak-Boy? Are you too spaced on your drugs? Now that you're a zombie does your girlfriend have to wipe your bum for you when you go to the loo?"

Rachel grabbed Paige's greasy ponytail and gave it a hard tug as a warning to keep her mouth shut in future, and Jamie finally lost it. He whirled round and shoved Rachel hard, pushing her away from Paige.

"Shut your mouth, Rachel Young, or I'll belt you so hard your tongue'll fall out!" he yelled. "Don't EVER touch Paige again."

Rachel might be rubbish at maths, but that didn't mean she wasn't smart. She'd seen Miss Morrison standing at the window stapling our Viking display work to the wall. As soon as the Dragon looked out to see what the shouting was about, Rachel toppled over, rolling around on the ground clutching her arm like it was broken.

"Stop it, Jamie!" she yelled at the top of her voice. "Leave me alone!"

"What on earth is going on here?" Miss Morrison came charging out of the doors and down the steps. "Jamie Lee! What have I told you about bullying Rachel?"

"It wasn't me!" Jamie protested. "It was Rachel! She started it. She was—"

"I don't need to hear any more of your stories." Miss Morrison cut him off and glared at Paige, who'd just opened her mouth to back him up. Paige shut it again quickly. She might be getting a bit braver, but she was still a coward when it came to teachers.

"Lauren, take Rachel to the office and ask Mrs Baird to look at her arm. Elin, what's been going on here?" Miss Morrison turned to me to get the true story. My reputation might not be perfect any more because of Jamie, but I was still her favourite. "Has Jamie been bullying Rachel again?"

Out of the corner of my eye I could see Rachel holding up a fist as she fake-limped away, daring me to tell the truth. Jamie was shaking his head behind the Dragon's back, begging me not to lie.

It was obvious what I had to say.

"Yes Miss Morrison," I nodded, "it was Jamie's fault. He started it."

I bit my lip and put my head down so I couldn't see the hurt expression on Jamie's face. I'd told so many lies about him now that I'd lost count, and I'd never be able to balance them with truths even if I was totally honest for the rest of my life.

If only I could find a way to turn Jamie back into the Monster, then maybe I wouldn't feel so bad about hurting him.

28

Jamie

I'll have to go to Miss Morrison's 'lunchtime homework club' again today because of Elin. It's a stupid thing to call it, I mean, it's not homework if we do it in school, is it? It's OK though cos I need peace and quiet to finish my book report, and it's easier to think when I've got the classroom mostly to myself. Miss Morrison helps me with my spelling and reading at the lunchtime club, so she knows now I'm not a completely stupid waste of space, even if she won't believe that I'm not a bully and a troublemaker.

I wish Elin would just stop hating me. When she tells lies about me it hurts worse than all of Rachel's poking fingers and nasty names put together.

Elin's sitting at the lunch table opposite mine right now, watching to see if I'll have a meltdown because she put another pack of cheese sticks in my lunchbox today. I know I ruined her birthday party, but that was ages ago, and I've given her every one of my Transformers stickers and most of my pocket money since then to make up for it.

Nothing I do seems to help. She still looks at me like I'm a monster.

I wish there was something I could do to make her like me. If I was rich and had an American Dream Life I could buy her those riding lessons she's always wanted, but where am I going to get the money for that, huh? I mean, I'd need at least a thousand pounds to…

Hey!

I nearly knock over my milkshake in excitement as the best idea ever whizzes into my brain at the speed of light. Miss Morrison told me this morning I was really good at science and I should enter the science fair. If I got picked to represent our school at the Glasgow Science Centre in May, and then I *won*, I could buy Elin all the riding lessons she wanted! She'd stop hating me, Dad would be really proud, Liz would like me for real instead of just pretending, and we'd be a proper family and live happily ever after!

In my rush to finish my food and get to the lunchtime club where I'll have peace and quiet to plan my experiment, I don't notice I've grabbed a cheese stick instead of a fruit straw, and I take a big bite of orange earwax before I can stop myself.

Argh!

I spit it out and take a swig of strawberry milkshake to take the taste away. Before I can start getting stressed by the slimy cheese worms wriggling about at the bottom of my lunchbox, Paige fishes them out and hands me a couple of Jammie Dodgers wrapped in an empty crisp packet instead.

"Here, I like cheese sticks. You can have my biscuits."

"Thanks," I grin. Paige knows all the things that wind me up, and she's helped me avoid more meltdowns than I can count. My medication's working properly now that I take a lower dose, and I don't get tired and fuzzy-headed any more, so I can finally think straight again. No, better than that, in the morning when we do maths and reading it's like the extra TV channels and static in my brain are a lot quieter and I can focus on what I'm doing. I know I'm not fixed like I'd hoped I'd be, but I don't feel quite so distracted for a few hours every day, and that makes me happier than I've been for years.

I can start to feel my meds wearing off after lunch though, and that's when I have to be extra careful not to let Rachel and Lauren wind me up. Paige is helping me with that, in lots of little ways no one else would ever think of.

"Here you go, two Mad Jamie Specials," I say like I'm a waiter in a restaurant, handing over the sandwiches I made for her last night. Paige loves my peanut butter, jam and whipped cream sandwiches. They're her best thing.

I bet Elin would love them too if she'd just try one.

She looks kind of lonely sitting over there by herself. No one's talking to her, and she's reading the label on her juice carton and pretending she doesn't care, but I think deep down she really does.

I turn round to tell Paige that maybe tomorrow we should ask Elin to sit with us, but when I see she's wearing one of my cheese sticks like a moustache I crack up laughing so hard I forget all about it. Rachel's on lunch duty today and comes over to see what's going on, and when she's looking at me, Paige waggles a cheese stick about behind her back till it breaks and falls on the floor. I pretend my milkshake went down the wrong way and I was just choking really loud, and Rachel steps on the cheese stick when she's walking away and goes stomping about with a big bit of smelly cheese stuck to the bottom of her shoe.

That makes me smile all afternoon.

By the time I run home I'm so hungry I could almost eat a cheese mountain, and my head's buzzing with ideas for my science project.

"Dad! Dad!" I yell as I race down the hall and go crashing into the kitchen. "You'll never guess what Miss Morrison said in school today!"

Elin's at the kitchen table reading a book. She looks up at me sharply like she's worried I'm going to tell on her for lying to the teacher and getting me detention.

"Remember that Junior Science Fair we got the leaflet about?" I tell Dad. "In May at the Glasgow Science Centre? All the schools are being asked for their best entries, and Miss Morrison announced that the judges are coming to our school at the end of this month! I always get top marks in science, so if I work hard I might get picked to represent our school!"

I can see Elin scowling at me, but I'm too excited to pay her any attention. I can tell she doesn't like the thought of not being the best at something, but it's not like she's interested in science, is it? She never wants to do any experiments with me, she never comes on bug hunts with me and Paige, and she doesn't ever watch the Discovery Channel with me, even though I always tell her when all the best programmes are on and offer to make her popcorn so she doesn't get hungry.

"That's great, Jamie!" Dad grins. It's a real smile, not one of the tired ones I saw a lot of before Christmas. He's been way happier since the doctor cut my medication in half and stopped me walking round like the undead. He wanted the old me back even more than I did. "Let me know what you need for it and we'll go shopping on Sunday while Elin's at her gran's with her dad, OK?"

"OK!" I grin back and give him a high five. Dad's hospital shifts changed back after the New Year. It's great having him at home again when I come back from school. Liz is nice, but she always tells me to do my homework first before I make my Mad Jamie Specials, and sometimes I get so hungry when the medication wears off I want to rip my homework jotter into little pieces and eat the pages.

"Hey Elin, are you going to enter the science competition?" I ask, banging about with plates and jars of jam and peanut butter.

Elin doesn't answer. She's biting her pencil and looking upset. I don't know what to do to cheer her up. I've tried everything I can think of to make her like me, so maybe I should just leave her alone like she says.

"Have you got any idea what you're going to do for your science project?" Dad asks me, taking a big bite of one of my sandwiches and making me laugh when he gets cream on his chin.

"Have I got any ideas?" I grin. "I'm the Sandwich Man – ideas are my best thing!"

29

Elin

"I'll get that, Mum. You go and make sure Jamie's put his uniform on. He doesn't listen to me in the morning."

"Thanks Elin, you're such a good girl. It's two capsules, remember?" Mum handed the medication bottle to me and went hurrying down the hall to make sure Jamie was ready for school. She had a big budget report to present in work this morning, and she couldn't afford to be even five minutes late.

This was the chance I'd been waiting for.

I opened the bottle and took two capsules out, holding them up to the light and examining them. They were all that was standing between me and my real family. It was funny that something so small could make the difference between Jamie being an out-of-control nightmare and the winner of our class's science quiz every week. The only way to get rid of him and Paul and get my family back was to let the Monster loose again.

And that meant telling the biggest lie I'd ever told.

I broke open the capsules the same way Mum did every morning, but instead of sprinkling the little white balls inside over a spoonful of peanut butter, I poured them into the bin. I spread some more peanut butter over the top of the spoon to make it look as if I'd buried the white balls inside, then I left the opened capsules on the counter by the sink where Mum could see them.

I put the medication bottle carefully back in the cupboard, sat down at the breakfast table, and waited.

In another thirty seconds there was a pounding of bare feet on the carpet and Jamie came charging down the hall and stampeding into the kitchen like a wild buffalo. He threw himself down at the table, took a big gulp of orange juice, shoved the spoonful of peanut butter into his mouth and swallowed without even looking at it. Then he began wolfing down his toast and talking at top speed about a dream he'd had last night where he was our class teacher and we spent all term building a giant rocket ship to take us to Mars.

I pretended I was just ignoring him as usual, but I was really watching him carefully out of the corner of my eye. Jamie ate food way too fast to even taste it most of the time, and that's what I was counting on.

He was so busy describing his rocket blasting off from the school launch pad that he didn't notice the peanut butter he'd swallowed tasted way better than usual. Jamie practically ate his food whole, but when it came to those little yellow capsules he couldn't bear to swallow them. Doctor Reid told Paul and Mum it was OK to break them open and sprinkle them in jam or peanut butter, just as long as Jamie didn't chew them. The little white balls slowly released the medication into his system through the day to keep him calmer and more focused.

Only today there'd be no medication keeping Jamie's temper in check.

It was time to wake the Monster and see just how loud he could roar.

After a few days of missed medication, Jamie was struggling to finish his history project and arguing with the other boys on the football pitch at break. Today we were supposed to be doing our maths workbooks until lunch, but Jamie couldn't concentrate. His eyes were darting everywhere like a wasp was buzzing round his head, and his hands and feet were all twitchy and restless. He'd accidentally kicked Darren under the table four times, and Darren had made it clear Jamie wouldn't be welcome at his house at the weekend to play computer games if it happened again.

Come on, I thought, watching him chew his pencil so hard it broke in two. *Just a few more distractions and he'll be ready to explode.*

"Are you OK?" Paige whispered for about the billionth time.

"I'm fine!" Jamie snapped. "Stop asking me that!"

Paige looked hurt and hid her face behind her workbook. I felt sorry for her for a moment, but then I remembered why I was doing this.

Jamie needs to be the Monster again or I'll never get rid of him and get my real family back, I reminded myself. *I can't feel bad for him or anyone else. I have to stay strong, like the Perfect Princess.*

Just then Jamie caught sight of my pencil case full of interesting things to play with. I'd deliberately filled it with a collection of my most tempting stationery. I could see his hands were itching to touch the glittery pens and pencil sharpeners in the shape of cherry cupcakes. As soon as his fingertips made contact with the nearest pen, I made sure all hell broke loose.

"Hey!" I shouted. "Stop touching my things!"

Jamie jerked back like he'd been stung, accidentally giving Darren another karate kick to the shin.

"Ow!" he yelled. "Cut it out you little freak, or I'll break your stupid head!"

"What's the problem here?" Miss Morrison came marching over, hands on her hips and her mouth drawn into a thin little line.

"Jamie keeps distracting us," I sighed dramatically. "It's really hard to get any work done."

Jamie opened his mouth to protest, but everyone at the table apart from Paige immediately jumped on the 'blame Jamie for breathing' bandwagon before he could get a word in edgeways.

"Jamie, what's the problem?" Miss Morrison snapped. She wasn't in a good mood this morning. Jamie had spilled his water bottle on her handbag when he was running from the sink after break, and her mobile phone got all wet. She wasn't going to tolerate any more bad behaviour from him today.

The Dragon picked up his maths workbook and flicked through it, and I could see her nostrils flaring like fire was about to come shooting out.

"You haven't done a single sum all morning! Are you deliberately trying to get into trouble?"

Jamie clamped his hands over his ears, the way he did when the stress got too much for him and he wanted to escape. It wasn't a very good way to hide from the stares and sniggers of the rest of the class who were waiting for his meltdown.

Just one more tiny push, that's all it would take.

Just one more—

"Are you listening to me, Jamie? Take your hands off your ears!"

Miss Morrison put a hand on his arm to calm him down, and Jamie completely lost it. He jumped up and grabbed his maths workbook, tearing it in two.

"I hate maths! It's STUPID! I hate this class!"

Before Miss Morrison could stop him, he'd raced out of the door, and we could hear his footsteps echoing down the corridor towards the gym hall. The Dragon heaved a big sigh like the fire she'd been ready to breathe had been unexpectedly put out, and marched after him.

As soon as she was gone everyone started whispering, and the classroom sounded like a hive of buzzing bees. I could feel a pair of eyes boring into the back of my head, but when I turned round it wasn't Rachel who was glaring at me, it was Paige. She'd stopped gazing after Jamie with her big concerned eyes, and was staring at me instead. For once, she didn't look like she wanted to be my friend.

I put my head down and tried to ignore her, burying the guilt down deep inside with all of my anger and frustration. I couldn't stop now, I *had* to win this war. I had to prove to Miss

Morrison that I was still the best pupil in the whole school and deserved the place at the science fair, and I had to prove to Dad that I was still his perfect daughter.

No matter what I did though, I'd never be able to prove to myself that I wasn't an awful person for what I was doing to Jamie.

Jamie

"Come on Jamie, you're nearly there, just a couple more lines," Dad says.

I heave a big sigh and fight the urge to chuck my marker pen off the wall.

I HATE writing almost as much as I hate cheese. I don't see why I have to handwrite all these stupid display signs, but Dad says the whole point of a science fair is that everyone can read about how you carried out your experiment. I'm pretty sure any idiot could look at my crystal garden and taste my rock candy and work out for themselves what I've done, but since I'm not thinking too straight these days I'll take Dad's word for it.

If it wasn't for all of Dad's help I would've given up on this science project weeks ago.

My brain's completely broken again, and I'm in so much trouble in class that if I don't win a place for our school in the science fair then I'll probably get expelled. I thought I was getting better, but I was obviously just kidding myself. There's no medicine that can fix me, no cure for my meltdowns. I'm always going to be Mad Jamie the Freak-Boy, and Mum was right to run a zillion miles away to America to get away from me.

I just wish there was somewhere I could run to get away from myself.

I don't know why my medication isn't working any more. The school's been ringing Dad and Liz every day about my behaviour, and I've had to go to the lunchtime homework club so many times I might as well just pack up and go and live in Miss Morrison's handbag. I've been sent home twice for fighting with Darren, and last week I got suspended from the football team, so no more dreams of playing in the World Cup for me.

I heard Liz talking on the phone to the head teacher the other day. He wants to get a special tutor in so I can have lessons on my own and not disturb anyone. It's like I'm a disease that everyone wants to quarantine so I won't infect the world with my craziness.

It doesn't matter what they try. There's no cure for being me.

"Great!" Dad gives me his biggest, most encouraging smile and moves my pen a bit so I don't go so far off the card that I start writing on the table. "Last line Jamie, then you've finished."

"Can't I just type it up on the computer and print it?" I whine, my hand starting to cramp in protest. "Everyone else will have theirs typed up, even Elin, and her handwriting's super-neat."

"Exactly," Dad grins. "The judges want to see that you've done the experiments all by yourself, and you clearly have. Most of the other kids' parents will have done their work for them, so your display will stand out a mile."

He doesn't smile much these days, so I finish writing for his sake, despite having serious doubt about the judges wanting to see my big loopy letters scrawled over the display cards.

"Done!" I announce, flinging the black marker down and vowing to throw the whole tub of pens in the bin as soon as Dad's back is turned. "That's everything, isn't it?" I shuffle the last display card into the pack and put it into my schoolbag without needing to be reminded. I don't want to leave anything behind tomorrow morning. This science competition is too important.

Dad's already helped me pack my crystal garden displays and rock candy trees into boxes ready to take to school. They're stacked neatly by the door, waiting to be put in Liz's car. While I was writing the last card, Dad was hanging up my school uniform on my wardrobe door and laying out my school shoes. He wants to make sure nothing spoils my big day tomorrow.

He knows how much winning this competition means to me. He just doesn't know the real reason why I want to win.

Liz and Dad are arguing about me every night now. Liz wants to take me back to the doctor to get my medication dose increased, and Dad wants everyone to stop blaming me for everything. Elin wants rid of me so badly I can even see her robot laser eyes burning a hole in the back of my head when I'm not looking. If I can just win that thousand pounds and buy Elin riding lessons, she'll finally like me, Liz will think I'm a nice person instead of a monster, and we can all live happily ever after.

It feels like I'm trying to win a war rather than just a science fair.

"That's us all set," Dad smiles. It's another tired smile, but if I look really hard there's a big helping of pride mixed into it as well. He knows how hard I've worked on this project, since he's sat with me every night for weeks while I've cried and shouted and fretted and fussed over getting my experiments done. He's the best dad in the whole world.

He doesn't deserve a monster son like me.

"How about we celebrate with a round of jam specials, hey Sandwich Man?"

We'll have the kitchen to ourselves. Liz will probably be in Elin's room all night helping her finish her butterfly project. I wish we could have all worked together, but no one except Dad wants to be in the same room as me any more.

"Aren't you bored of eating my sandwiches?" I ask. "Mum never liked them, and Liz says you shouldn't encourage me to eat so much sugar."

"Jamie, there's only one thing in the whole world I love more than your sandwiches," Dad says.

"What's that? Chicken nuggets? Chocolate cake? Please don't say it's cheese or I'll disown you!"

"No, it's you of course," Dad laughs, nudging me and making me giggle when I nearly fall off the end of the bed. "Race you to the kitchen. Last one there has to do the washing-up!"

31

Elin

"Done!"

I stepped back and admired my butterfly display. The coloured foil wings shimmered like jewels in the sunlight, just like the ones Dad made me in our last summer together. My tropical rainforest scene was so big I needed to use up a whole pack of thumb tacks to pin it to the assembly hall wall. A couple of girls from 7A complained I was using their space, but their entry was just a rubbish papier mâché volcano they copied off the internet, so none of the classroom assistants helping us paid any attention to them.

My project was perfect. Everyone thought so.

"That's stunning, Elin! You definitely deserve to win," one of the assistants said, stopping to look.

I grinned and finished pinning my neat printouts to the wall with a description of each butterfly. There was also a central poster explaining how butterfly wings work – that was the science bit of my project – but it didn't seem very important when my display was so pretty.

The judges were going to love it.

The break-time bell rang just as I put up my last display card, and a big group of teachers came in to have a look at the entries on their way to the staffroom. Most of the other kids headed out to the playground, but I hung around for a bit, pretending to straighten some of the cards and waiting for more compliments.

I waited.

And waited.

When they didn't come I looked round.

The teachers were all gathered at a table further down the hall, looking at Jamie's display. He'd already run off at top speed to go and wreak havoc in the playground, so I was the one who heard everything the teachers had to say about his entry.

"It's really impressive, isn't it? This'll definitely be the one the judges pick to represent our school."

"He's obviously done it all by himself, not like some of these displays."

"Jamie's light years ahead of the rest of the class in science," Miss Morrison said. "If that boy could just concentrate on his work in school he'd have a bright future ahead of him."

"Oh! Elin, are you still here?" Mr Robertson from 7A looked round as I tiptoed past on my way out. Behind him I caught a glimpse of Jamie's science experiment, and my breath caught painfully in my throat.

It was brilliant.

I hadn't paid any attention to what chemicals he was mixing in his room these last few weeks, or what he'd been cooking up in pots in the kitchen with Paul. I was so focussed on my own display I didn't even look to see what he was unpacking onto his table this morning. There was an amazing miniature garden, with blue, green and pink crystals growing on pebbles and sprouting from tiny plant pots. They were all shapes and sizes, some long and thin like needles, some tall and rectangular, and some tiny like grains of sugar. Each type of crystal had a card next to it explaining its properties and how it was made, and a whole bunch of other information I was too far away to read despite Jamie's giant messy handwriting.

At the end of the table was a big rock-candy tree, with lollipop sticks covered in boiled sugar crystals, and a sign next to it saying *Taste me!* On the wall behind it was a poster covered in rock-candy recipes and photographs showing each stage of the crystal-growing process.

My stomach gave a sick lurch when I realised the teachers were right.

Jamie was going to win.

Jamie was going to be the one to represent our school at the Junior Science Fair in the Glasgow Science Centre in May.

It was so unfair I wanted to scream.

Instead I forced myself to smile and said, "I'm just finished setting up now. I'm going out to the playground."

"You've put a lot of work into that." Mr Robertson nodded at my butterfly display. "It's lovely."

"It's more of an art display than a science project though, Elin," Miss Morrison added. "Don't be too disappointed if the judges don't pick it as the winner. They're going to be looking for the best experiment, not the prettiest pictures."

The teachers nodded their agreement and carried on discussing Jamie's display in hushed voices. I went back to class to get my jacket, but instead of heading out to the playground, I went to the girls' toilets instead. I felt so sick with anger and jealousy I wanted to throw up, but that wasn't why I was hiding there.

I knew what I had to do.

I clutched the edge of the sink and stared at my pale face in the mirror. There were dark shadows under my eyes and my lips were cracked from all the nervous chewing. I was so stressed about being caught messing with Jamie's medication that I hadn't slept properly in weeks, and the guilt pains were so bad my stomach was in knots every morning.

So far it had all been worth it. Jamie was the Monster again, and Mum and Paul were arguing so much about his behaviour they were on the verge of splitting up. One more major blow-up and it would all be over. I'd get my real family back, and we'd live happily ever after.

But only if Jamie didn't represent our school at the science fair.

If he proved he could be top of the school at something despite his behaviour, then I'd never get rid of him.

My fairy-tale ending was slipping out of my grasp, and there was only one way I could get it back.

"You can do it," I whispered to my reflection. "You have to!"

I waited till I was sure the teachers would all be in the staffroom, then I slipped out and headed back to the assembly hall.

Jamie was never going to forgive me for what I was about to do.

But was I ever going to be able to forgive myself?

Jamie

"But I need to *peeeeee*!" I insist, dancing on the spot and trying to show the playground supervisor how urgent my case is.

"You were supposed to go before you came out! There's only another ten minutes of break left, can't you wait?"

Miss Finlay doesn't like us going in and out at break time and 'getting up to mischief', as she calls it, but one look at my pained face is enough to confirm I'll cause way more trouble if she doesn't let me back in.

"Fine, come straight back out though, do you hear me, Jamie? No detours or mucking about at the water fountain."

She swipes her keycard to open the security lock, and I run back in to go to the loo before my bladder explodes. I don't know why I'm so desperate to pee – I was so busy setting up my science display this morning I didn't even remember to fill up my water bottle.

It's still sitting on my desk.

My classroom's not *that* far from the boys' toilet and the water fountain. Maybe I should just fill it while I'm here…

I run back to class and fetch it, nearly knocking the janitor down in the corridor and spilling water on the floor when I hold my water bottle the wrong way up.

"Jamie, shouldn't you be outside?" The head teacher frowns at me as he walks past. He's taking three people to the staff room. They look important. They must be the science fair judges.

For one mad second I think about bowing to them like they're royalty, and then I have to clamp my hand over my mouth to stop myself laughing out loud at how funny that would look.

"I'm just going to the toilet," I mumble through a mouthful of fingers, and then I run off before I can get into trouble for turning the corridor into the River Clyde.

We're doing a project about Scottish rivers in class just now. It's not as much fun as the Vikings, but that's only because Miss Morrison didn't listen to my suggestion about making a model Viking boat to go sailing on the Clyde. She said we'd already made a boat, and I said the cardboard boat stuck on the wall was a bit rubbish, and she said I was cheeky and I'd get extra homework if I wasn't careful.

Why isn't it cheeky when Miss Morrison tells me my handwriting's rubbish then?

Maybe I should give *her* homework when she makes me rewrite my science reports.

She's in a good mood with me for once as she thinks my science fair entry is brilliant, even though the writing on my cards is all over the place. I'm so nervous and excited and worried all at the same time at the thought of winning that my stomach feels like I've swallowed Elin's whole butterfly display in one gulp.

The judges will probably pick her entry, even though it's not a proper science project, just a lot of pretty pictures. Everything about Elin is pretty, from her neat handwriting and super-clean clothes to her stupid painted pottery collection. Teachers love her. They think she's perfect.

They don't know she tells lies and says hurtful things when they're not listening.

She's not so perfect on the inside.

Not like Paige.

I'm playing with the taps and feeling bad that Paige is avoiding me after all the times I lost my temper and yelled at her, when Steven puts his head round the door.

"Didn't you hear the bell, Jamie? Break time's over. Miss Morrison's looking for you. She says you have to come *right now!*"

He looks excited, like he knows something he's not telling me.

I wonder if it's something bad, and the sick feeling in my stomach gets worse when he leads me down the corridor to the assembly hall instead of back to class.

"Is the judging finished already?" I ask. "That was quick!"

Steven shoots me a look that's half nervous and half sympathetic. It's the kind of look you give someone when their pet dog's been run over and you don't want to be the one to tell them. But I don't have a pet dog, so I don't know why I'm getting the look.

"The head teacher wants all of us who entered the science fair competition to come to the assembly hall," he says, without really answering my question.

Steven's got a pet dog. Maybe it's his dog that's been run over.

There's lots of teachers and a bunch of classroom assistants in the hall. They should all be in class now that break time's over, and Mr Conway the head teacher should be in his office eating Hobnobs with his super-important guests. He's not though. He's standing there with his hands on his hips staring at me like I'm the driver who's just run over Steven's dog.

"Jamie, why would you do this?" he asks. "What were you thinking?"

"Do what?" I blink. "I haven't done—" And then I see what they're all looking at.

My display's been completely smashed.

The table's lying on its side and the crystals have been trampled so hard into the floor all that's left of them is piles of coloured powder. My rock candy tree's been pulled apart and the boiled sugar lollipops are strewn around in bits. The display cards I spent so long writing have been ripped to pieces and the photographs are all torn.

There's nothing left of my entry.

I'm not going to win a place at the science fair now.

For a long moment I can't speak. All the air's been sucked out of my lungs. I stare back at Mr Conway with my mouth open, waiting for him to tell me it's all just a big joke.

He doesn't. He just asks again, "Why did you do it, Jamie?"

"I didn't!" My voice doesn't come out above a whisper. "It wasn't me."

"Don't lie, Jamie, not about this." Miss Morrison's towering over me with her badger hair and coffee breath, and I'm so full of rage I can barely keep the peanut butter toast I had for breakfast down.

"Miss Finlay let you back in at break, and the janitor saw you in the corridor just outside."

"I saw you myself," Mr Conway says. "We've asked all the other boys and girls and you were the only one in here at break. Why would you destroy your own experiments, Jamie? It's completely senseless."

I look round the hall like I'm searching for someone to rescue me, but no one offers to help. Paige isn't here. She isn't entering the science fair. Her mum can't afford to buy any craft stuff. She can't save me from the ten-ton bomb of rage that's ticking down to zero in my head. Everyone's staring right at me, waiting for me to explode.

Everyone except Elin.

Her eyes are on the floor, and she's clenching her hands so tight her knuckles are white. Today she isn't hard to read. The guilt's written all over her face.

Her betrayal hits me so hard I nearly fall over.

"It was Elin!" I gasp. "She did it!"

Elin's head snaps up, her cheeks flaming red. "Of course I didn't!" she says, too quick and too loud. "I'd never do anything like that."

"She's lying!" I yell. "She's the one who ruined everything!"

"Elin doesn't lie," Miss Morrison frowns. "I'm afraid you're the one with the history of that, Jamie."

There's no way for me to win. Elin has them all wrapped so tightly round her little finger she could pull my experiment to pieces right in front of them and they'd still think it was me. I can't believe they're so blind. I can't believe *I've* been so blind.

I thought if I was nice to her for long enough she'd stop hating me and we could be a real family. I spent weeks working on my science project so I'd have a chance of winning enough money to buy her riding lessons and make her dreams come true. I forgave her even though she lied to Miss Morrison and Dad and Liz about me time and time again.

I even trusted her with my medication every morning.

Wait.

My medication...

I've been feeling all wrong for weeks.

Ever since Elin started giving me my medication instead of Liz.

The time bomb of anger goes off, and all of a sudden I'm screaming and crying and lashing out at the classroom assistants who try to stop me reaching Elin's butterfly display.

I don't want their sympathy or their soothing words.

I want revenge.

33

Elin

If Miss Finlay hadn't got between Jamie and my butterfly display then it would've been torn to pieces.

It didn't matter in the end. I didn't win a place at the science fair.

The sick feeling in the pit of my stomach had been getting worse all day, and now it was mixed with a heavy sense of dread as I dragged my feet all the way home. I didn't want to face Jamie and his accusing eyes. I didn't want to lie to Mum and Paul about what happened, but what choice did I have?

My fairy tale had gone badly wrong and now I was the Monster who didn't deserve a happy ending. If Dad ever found out what I'd done he'd be so disappointed he wouldn't want to see me again. I had to keep lying, no matter how much it hurt.

I crossed the street to our house just in time to see Mum's car heading away on the main road. I slowed down even more when I saw that Paul's car wasn't sitting in our drive. He wasn't home from work yet, and Mum had to go back to the office for a meeting. That meant Jamie was in the house all by himself.

The teachers had tried to calm him down, but when that didn't work they called Mum to come and pick him up and take him home. I was in class pretending to type up a book report when she came, but I could see her in the corridor talking in a hushed voice to Miss Morrison. Mum looked so stressed and upset I wanted to cry.

I knew it was the last straw for her, and I'd won the final battle. I'd proved that Jamie didn't belong with us. But now it felt like a hollow victory. It felt like I'd turned myself inside out and all the nastiness and jealousy that had been eating me up ever since Dad left was oozing out for everyone to see.

I didn't deserve to get my family back now.

There were funny banging noises coming from somewhere inside the house as I walked up the drive. It sounded like Jamie was taking his anger out on the punch bag Paul had given him for Christmas. Now wasn't a good time to disturb him. I didn't want him getting me and the punch bag mixed up. Paul would be home any minute. Maybe I should just sit on the doorstep and wait for him.

I put my schoolbag down and leaned against the front door, trying to ignore the banging, and listening instead to the sounds of the cars passing on the road and the birds singing in the trees. It was almost the Easter holidays. Soon I'd be off school and wouldn't have to hang my head in shame every time Miss Morrison looked at me. I could hardly believe I'd just stood there and let her blame Jamie for what I did. I could hardly believe how awful I'd become.

The banging stopped suddenly, and for a long moment there was only silence.

Then another sound came from inside the house, a soft snuffling that got louder when I pressed my ear against the door and listened. Jamie was still crying after what I'd done to him this morning. The image of his shocked face when he realised I was the one who destroyed all his hard work was burned into my brain.

He'd believed all my lies. He'd trusted me to give him his medication. He'd never given up trying to make friends with me. And that made me feel even worse.

Maybe it wasn't too late. Maybe I could still fix this. Maybe I could tell him it wasn't me, that it was Darren, or Steven, or Rachel, or any of the other kids in our class who'd entered the science fair. Maybe I could get him to swallow one more lie the way he swallowed my spoonfuls of medicine-free peanut butter.

I stuck my key in the lock and opened the front door, nearly tripping over something sprawled on the doormat. It was Jamie, sitting in the hallway with his back against the wall and his face red with tears.

I hesitated for a long moment, wondering whether it would be safer just to run. Jamie looked up at me, and I tensed, waiting for the angry words. They didn't come. All that came out of Jamie's mouth was a whisper I didn't catch until he repeated it.

"I'm sorry," he whimpered. "I didn't mean it. I was so angry."

Jamie was apologising to *me*? It was so weird that for a long moment I didn't know what to say. Then the sick feeling in my stomach tightened into a knot of fear. Something was horribly wrong, and I wasn't sure I wanted to find out what it was.

"Jamie, what have you done?"

Jamie drew his knees up to his chest and hid his face. I'd destroyed his science fair entry and spoiled his chances of representing our school, but that wasn't why he was crying. They weren't angry tears, they were guilty ones. He'd done something so awful he was too upset to look at me.

"Jamie Lee, tell me what's going on or I swear I'll—"

I stopped and looked down the hallway. Something bad had happened. Something that made Jamie so ashamed he couldn't look me in the eye.

That was when I noticed my bedroom door was open.

Jamie had been in my room.

34

Jamie

"Don't go in there!" I beg, trying to catch Elin's leg as she hurries past. "Wait till Dad comes home! Please!"

Elin isn't listening. She's running down the hallway now, straight into the eye of the storm. The worst of my fury might've passed, but there's no escaping the devastation left in its wake.

Elin stops in the doorway, clamping a hand over her mouth when she sees the destruction. I pick myself up and shuffle closer, half afraid she's going to whirl round and punch me right in the head.

She's too shocked to move though. She's too stunned to even cry. She looks exactly the same way I did when I saw what she'd done to my science display. I wanted to hurt her for what she did. I wanted her to feel just as bad as I did.

Now all I want is to turn the clock back.

"How could you do this?" Elin's voice comes out in a sob, and she stares round her room with eyes so wide they look like they'll come popping out of her head any second. She can't believe what she's seeing. All of her carefully painted knights and castles are smashed to pieces. Every single piece of pottery and ceramic I could get my hands on has been thrown against the wall and stomped into the carpet. I've broken her paint boxes and snapped her brushes, and there's a big crack down her wardrobe mirror where I flung her computer.

She can replace the mirror and the computer, but she can't replace the ornaments she's spent years collecting and hours and hours painting. Every single thing in her room is smashed beyond repair, just like my science experiment. It seemed fair when I was destroying it all. It seemed like justice.

Now it just seems cruel, and I'm sick with regret.

"NO! Not Athena!" Elin screeches at the top of her voice and runs to gather up the pieces of the little white horse I've shattered into so many bits you can't even tell what it used to be. She sits there on the carpet, gasping for breath so hard I think she's going to faint.

I hide my head in my hands and count to one hundred, and by the time I move them again and take a peek, Elin's stopped gasping and is staring at me with so much hatred in her robot laser eyes I can feel my brain starting to fry.

"That's it! I can't take this any more!"

Elin slams her bedroom door in my face, wedging something up against it so I can't open it again. I can hear her banging and crashing about, opening and closing drawers and pulling things out of her wardrobe. At first I think she's cleaning up the mess, but every time she crosses the carpet there's a soft crunching sound as more and more pieces of china and pottery are crushed beneath her shoes.

"Elin?" I whimper, knocking on her door and trying to push against the heavy thing that's wedged on the other side. "Elin, I'm sorry, but you wrecked my science experiment too! You know how hard I worked on that. Dad'll be back soon, can you open the door and let me in?"

Elin ignores me. I don't know why I want her to let me in, or why being shut out in the hall scares me so much. It's like I know that things have spiralled way out of control and it's not just my science project and Elin's pottery that are broken beyond repair.

There's a big, nasty change coming, I can feel it.

I don't want to be locked out on the wrong side when it arrives.

Elin finishes what she's doing and finally comes stomping out again. She's carrying a rucksack and her mouth's so tight it looks like an elastic band about to snap. She marches past me and out the front door, and before I can catch her she's halfway down the street.

"Elin! Where are you going?" I call. I'm too scared to follow her. I'm tired and upset and confused and I just want my dad to come home.

"As far away from you as I can!" Elin yells back. Her eyes are flashing and her face is all scrunched up in a scowl but I think she's trying hard not to cry. "You want to live here? Fine! My house is all yours. You won the war. I lost. I'm leaving and I'm never coming back!"

"Elin! Wait!"

But she doesn't. She just keeps marching down the street, turning the corner without looking back and disappearing from sight. I hesitate in the driveway, looking back at the house and then up the street again. I can't decide whether to follow her or wait for Dad. Snap decisions are my trademark, but for the first time ever my brain isn't telling me what to do.

Dad'll be back any minute. He'll know how to fix this.

I sit down on the doorstep and wait, the knot of fear in my stomach getting tighter with each car that passes and doesn't turn in to our drive.

Elin really went off the deep end today, and I went jumping right in behind her.

I wonder which of us will be in the most trouble?

Is the mess I made of her room worse than her wrecking my science project? Is there a ten-point scale of destruction that adults use to decide who gets the most blame?

And what did she mean I've 'won the war'?

How can I win a game I didn't even know I was playing?

Part Four

Taking Flight

35

Elin

"Elin! What are you doing here?"

Gran looked so surprised when she opened the door and saw me standing on her doorstep that I thought she was going to have a heart attack. The carefully prepared story I'd been rehearsing over and over on the bus all the way to Whitburn went flying out of my head, and I flung my arms round Gran's neck and choked back a sob.

"He's ruined everything, Gran!" I cried. "I can't go back there now, not ever! Can I stay here with you? Please?"

Even now I was still blaming Jamie for the trouble I'd caused. I didn't know what else to do. The truth was too painful, and I pushed it as far away as I could.

"Aw pet, what's happened? Come in and get warm and I'll phone your mum."

"No! I don't want her knowing I'm here." I didn't want to see her disappointed face when she found out everything I'd done.

"Well at least come in from the cold and have some hot chocolate," Gran said, glancing back up the stairs as though she was afraid someone would hear me. My imagination must've been playing tricks on me. Gran never had any visitors apart from me and Mum and Dad.

"Is Dad here?" I asked hopefully, taking my shoes off and curling up on the sofa in the living room. Gran's soft cushions surrounded me like a big fabric hug, and I felt safe and protected. Nothing could hurt me here.

"Why do you ask that?" Gran sounded nervous, and her eyes darted to the hall door again.

"Just wondered," I yawned. I was so tired. Today had been the longest day of my life. "I thought I saw his overnight bag in the hall – the one he used to take on work trips before..."

Before he left and the Mutant came and ruined our lives and he gave up work to look after her.

He never gave up work when I was born.

Because Dad loves her more, whispered a voice deep in my mind.

Shut up! I thought angrily. *You don't get to tell my story.*

"It's just us," Gran said. "You sit there pet, and I'll get some hot chocolate to warm you up, then you can tell me all about it."

She smiled her familiar, reassuring smile, but there was something wrong with the corners of her mouth and the smile didn't touch her eyes. It was the same wary smile Paige Munro used to give me at break time when she asked if I wanted to play with her.

It was strangely cold for an April evening. The central heating was on and Gran had her gas fire turned up almost full, but I was still shivering. My head was spinning, thoughts of Jamie's medication and his ruined science display and my shattered ornament collection going round and round until I felt dizzy.

Remembering the bombsite Jamie had made of my room made me so anxious I could barely breathe. I used to be so good at keeping things neat, and now I didn't even know where to begin to clean up the mess.

It wasn't just Athena who was broken beyond repair. The mess I'd made of my family was going to be just as impossible to fix.

It's Jamie's fault! I tried to tell myself as Gran warmed the milk in the kitchen. *He started all of this. I just did what I had to do.*

Miss Morrison might still believe my lies, but I couldn't convince myself any more.

The only thing I had left to cling to now was Gran and her Enchanted Cottage that never changed. I looked round the room at the familiar photos on the mantelpiece and pictures on the wall, and for one long moment I felt safe and protected from the chaos of my life.

Then I realised the pictures had all changed too.

"There you go, pet." Gran came back in and tried to hand me a steaming mug of chocolate, but I barely glanced at it. I was too busy staring at the pictures Gran had sitting on the mantelpiece.

There in the middle was a photo of a little girl. Dad was giving her a piggyback, playing my favourite game of horses and knights. It was exactly the way I remembered it from when I was younger.

Only the girl in the photo wasn't me.

"Who's THAT?" I demanded, jumping up and waving the picture at Gran.

She hesitated, her eyes going wide and guilty. She looked just like Jamie had right before I discovered what he'd done to my ornament collection.

"It's, um, she's…" Gran didn't finish. She didn't need to. We both knew who it was. I looked round. Some of our other family pictures weren't where they usually were when I came to visit. They'd been replaced with pictures of Dad and Sue and Beth. Some of the photos even looked like they'd been taken in this very house. Beside the TV was a box full of toys, and the glittery photo album I'd found here last year was sitting open on the coffee table. I'd been so upset when I arrived that I hadn't noticed them.

"Gran, what's going on?"

I didn't want to believe what my eyes were telling me. I didn't want to hear that Gran had been lying to me.

Gran was my Fairy Godmother. She was supposed to be on *my* side.

"Look Elin, it's not what you think, it's just—"

Right at that moment I heard a padding of small feet on the stairs, and the hall door swung open.

"Granny?" a little girl asked, rubbing her eyes and looking up sleepily. "Is Daddy here?"

In that moment everything became crystal clear. Paul had replaced Dad in Mum's house and brought Jamie to take my place. Now the Mutant was in Gran's house replacing me. I didn't belong anywhere.

"How could you bring her here?" I cried. "How could you do this to me?"

"Now look here Elin, Beth's my granddaughter too," Gran frowned. She'd got her breath back and she sounded stern, like I was going to get a row rather than a sympathy hug. "This whole silly pantomime has gone on for long enough. Come and say hello to Beth, she's been dying to meet you."

Gran bent down to lift the little girl up, but by the time her knees had stopped creaking I'd already got my shoes back on, grabbed my bag and was escaping through the hall. I flung the front door open and went running down the street, ignoring Gran's worried shouts from the doorway.

"Elin! Come back! Where are you going?"

It was the second time I'd run away today.

All my safe spaces were gone, and now there was only one place left for me to go.

Don't look back! I told myself, my heart hammering in my chest in time with my feet pounding on the pavement. *Be brave, just like the princess in your story.*

I didn't feel brave running away from all my problems though. I felt angry and helpless and betrayed by everyone. But more than anything I just felt scared.

It was getting late and the streetlights looked like glowing yellow eyes against the inky sky, staring at me accusingly as I fled down the street. A car on the main road slowed down as it passed, the driver looking out of the window and honking her horn to get my attention.

"Are you alright, pet?" she called.

I cut down an alley to get away from her.

There was one other route, and that was through the Tangled Wood. It was only called that in my story, but I used to play there with Lindsay and Olivia after school. Back then it had been our very own adventure playground, with hollow trees to hide our secrets and blackberries growing on the thick bushes. Tonight it looked dark and scary, and I hesitated on the pavement. The overgrown path no longer seemed to invite me in the way it used to.

I heard a police siren wailing in the distance, and that made up my mind for me. What if Gran had called the police? Was running away against the law? Was I going to be in trouble for that as well as for what I did to Jamie's science fair entry?

I wasn't going to stick around long enough to find out.

I headed into the wood, pushing my way through the overgrown branches that blocked the path. I knew it was just a little patch of trees next to the swing park, but in my imagination it had grown to the size of a huge forest, filled with terrible creatures that were slithering through the dark towards me.

Don't stop now! I tried to tell myself. *You can face anything!*

But I wasn't a hero in real life, and I was very far from being a perfect fairy-tale princess. The sounds of the road had died away, and in their place were strange bird calls and the eerie whistling of the wind through the leaves.

Then I heard something even worse.

There were voices up ahead, coming from a group of teenagers in hoodies who were hanging about the clearing. Their laughter stopped when I stumbled into the light of the small campfire they'd lit. There was a long silence as they stared at me, then their faces relaxed again.

"It's alright, it's just a wee kid," one of the boys grinned.

I was too scared to feel reassured by their friendly smiles. I turned to run back the way I came, but my foot caught a tree root on the uneven path. I went tumbling into a bramble bush, cutting my hand badly and tearing my school jumper on the thorns.

"Are you OK?" one of the girls called, hurrying over to help me. I struggled up before she could reach me, choking back a sob and stumbling down the path clutching my aching hand to my chest.

I had to get to safety.

I had to go *home*.

36

Jamie

"This was a bad idea – one of us should have stayed at home in case she goes back there," Liz says, running her hands through her short hair again. She's done that so many times since Mrs Watts called to say Elin had run off to Whitburn that her hair's standing up in hedgehog spikes.

"I'll drive back with Jamie," Dad says. "If she turns up I'll call you and come back here to pick you up."

"What did you bring him here for anyway?" Liz mutters. She doesn't even look at me, so I know she's really mad. The only good thing about Elin running off is that now Liz has something more important to worry about than the demolition wreck I've made of Elin's room. I haven't told them about Elin messing with my meds yet. I can't get a word in over their constant yelling anyway.

"This isn't Jamie's fault," Dad says defensively. "Elin started this by ruining Jamie's science project. He spent weeks on that! She ran away because she's ashamed of what she did."

Uh-oh. Not this again.

"She ran away because Jamie destroyed all the things she's spent *years* making!" Liz snaps. "One little science project can't compare to the awful thing your son did!"

"I'm sick of you blaming Jamie for everything! He's bent over backwards to fit in with this family, and Elin's been nothing but mean to him since the day he arrived!"

"What do you expect? His behaviour's so appalling he's been making her life a misery! How can you expect her to—"

"Enough, you two!" Mrs Watts steps between them before I can sink through the carpet in shame. "I've just got Beth back to sleep, and I don't want her disturbed again. Now, *think*. Where might Elin have gone?"

"She'll have got the bus home," Dad says. "I'll go back with Jamie and check."

"No, not home, I'm sure she—" I begin, but Dad's not in the mood to listen to me right now either.

"We're going back Jamie, that's the end of it," he snaps, grabbing his car keys. "I'll phone the police again first to check if they have any updates for us."

"But I wasn't going to say—"

"She might've got on a bus to Edinburgh to see her dad," Liz frowns. "She always said she'd never go while Sue and Beth were there, but she might've changed her mind now she knows Beth's here. I'll give Adam a call."

"I don't think she—" is all I manage to get out before Mrs Watts interrupts me this time.

"She used to play with that girl Olivia Sinclair, remember? They used to be such good friends at school when you lived here.

Her mother's still in my coffee club at church— I'll call her and see if Elin's gone to their house."

"But—" I try again, but everyone walks off to make their calls and I'm left standing alone in the living room with my mouth flapping up and down.

I know where Elin went, I'm sure of it. The pictures above her bed of her old house in Whitburn were gone when she walked out, and I spent the whole drive here searching online street views on my phone to figure out which house it is. Maybe if I find her first then they'll all forgive me for making her run off, and things will go back to the way they were. The way things were was pretty awful, but it was still better than this.

I grab my jacket and head into the hall, closing the front door quietly behind me.

I'm a man on a mission.

It's the one chance I have left to keep my family from breaking beyond repair.

Running down the street in the dark makes me feel like a private detective in one of those TV shows. I have to track Elin down before something bad happens to her, but I have to break all the rules to do it. I'm already in the most trouble ever for wrecking her room, so running off now isn't going to make things worse, is it?

At least, I hope not.

I'm so busy peering in the gardens and shadows as I race past that I don't notice I've run straight onto a busy road until there's a thump and a horrible screeching of brakes right in my ear. It's only when I'm rolling on the ground that I realise the thump was my leg hitting the side of a van.

"God! Are you alright?" A man comes jumping out and runs over. My head's all muddled, and I have this weird idea that he's a police officer come looking for the rogue private detective who's breaking the rules, and before I can work out what's real and what's just make-believe, I'm giving him the thumbs up and escaping down an alley.

To keep going in the direction of Elin's old house, I have to choose between cutting though an abandoned swing park or a creepy forest that looks like something out of the werewolf horror film I watched the other night. I climb awkwardly over the fence into the park, hoping the werewolves all have better places to be tonight.

There's one swing still left in the frame, and I go and sit on it to catch my breath. Man-oh-man, that van was close to squashing me flat as a pancake. I wonder how big my bruise is going to be? The top of my leg's gone sort of numb, but when it wakes up it's going to register a definite ten on the scientific 'ouch' scale.

I swing back and forth for a bit, rubbing my leg to get the circulation going again and listening to the rusty chains squealing. Come to think of it, if someone was going to get eaten by horror-film monsters, this park would be a great place for it. There are walls on two sides, and a group of dodgy-looking teenagers who may or may not be werewolves laughing at the bus stop.

My leg's itching, which means it's waking up. I pull one side of my jeans down to find out if there's a bruise, but it's too dark to see and I realise standing in the middle of an abandoned park with my trousers down is not very detective-like.

"You alright, wee man?"

Uh-oh. The werewolves have spotted me and are crossing the road to the park. I pull my jeans up and gulp hard, backing away as the leader of the pack comes lumbering towards me.

There's nowhere left to run.

37

Elin

I was crying so hard by the time I reached my old house that I could barely see the road ahead.

I couldn't pretend I was the Perfect Princess who didn't shed a single tear any more, and I wasn't strong and fearless like her. I was cold and scared, and the cut on my hand was throbbing so much I felt dizzy. If that wasn't bad enough, I'd been stupid and selfish, and I'd ruined any chance my family had of being happy.

No wonder Dad and Gran loved Beth more than they loved me.

Shut up! I yelled at the nasty voice in my head, wishing I could turn the clock back and start all over again. Maybe this time I'd be nice to Jamie. I'd leave his science entry alone and let him represent our school, and the fairy-tale figures I'd spent years painting wouldn't be lying in pieces on my bedroom floor. I tried hard not to think about Athena. Losing my little painted horse hurt almost as much as seeing Beth at Gran's house.

I gulped back another sob and shoved my bleeding hand in my pocket, hiding in the shadows of a fir tree by the front garden, staring at the silhouette of my fairy-tale castle outlined against the night sky.

The lights were on in the living room. The people who'd stolen my old home were in. I'd have to be careful not to be seen. I took a deep breath and unfastened the latch on the side gate, trying not to make any noise. Then I tiptoed down the path, ducking along the fence so I wouldn't be spotted from the kitchen window. One last dash across the grass in the dark and finally I was at the shed that sat at the bottom of the back garden. This was my hideout, the only safe place in the world left for me to go.

It was only when I'd lifted off the rusty padlock and crept inside that I realised this last refuge had changed just as much as the rest of my life. The shed hadn't been cluttered like this when we were living here. I sat down on a big tin of paint and rested my chin on my knees, my head aching as all the memories of my past life flooded back.

Running away was the worst idea I'd ever had.

It was freezing, and the lawnmower and bike handles were poking into my back so hard I had to keep shifting around to try to get comfy. I was going to get absolutely filthy, and that worried me almost as much as the thought of Mum panicking when she found I was gone.

Dad had stored everything neatly in shelves and racks, and he painted it every summer with wood sealer so the rain wouldn't get in. Now the shed smelt damp and musty, and there was rust on the blades of the hedge shears that were piled in a box by the door. It used to be my favourite hiding place in all the world, and now a few more bad winters and it would be ready to fall down.

Yet another special thing had been destroyed by Mum and Dad's divorce. My happy ending was so far out of reach I couldn't even imagine it any more. We were never going to get our home back now.

This isn't your home any more.

The unwelcome voice in my head was getting louder. Or maybe now I'd stopped believing in my fairy story I was just paying more attention to it.

You have to go back to your real home before someone finds you here.

I looked out of the small window to the house at the other end of the garden. Lights were on in the kitchen now but the curtains were drawn, so I couldn't see more than a shadowy shape moving around inside. It was long past dinner time. Someone must be doing the dishes.

My stomach growled painfully and I put a hand over it to keep it quiet. I was starving. After what I did to Jamie's science fair display I hadn't felt like eating my packed lunch. I'd told the lunch monitor I felt sick, and she let me go straight out to the playground.

Everyone believed me when I told lies, but no one believed Jamie when he told the truth.

Maybe that's why I was too ashamed to go home. I'd have to admit all the lies I'd told since Jamie turned up on our doorstep, and I didn't think I could face Mum and Paul's disappointment, or the hurt on Jamie's puppy-dog face.

Suddenly the light from the kitchen was blotted out as a shadow passed by the shed window.

My breath caught in my throat, and I grabbed a small trowel from the garden toolbox. I had no idea what I was going to do with it, but my heart was pounding so loudly in my chest I couldn't think straight. Had someone seen me go into the shed? Had they called the police? Was I going to be in even more trouble?

The footsteps stopped outside, and for a long moment there was silence.

Then the door gave a painful creak and swung slowly open.

A figure stood in the doorway, framed in the dim glow from the kitchen light. I bit my lip to keep from crying out, backing as far as I could into the tangle of bikes and garden equipment.

The shadow stepped forward, and flicked on a torch. Its rays panned the inside of the shed, coming to rest on my feet sticking out from behind the lawnmower.

I'd been found.

38

Jamie

"There you are, Elin!" I grin, switching off my Transformers torch and closing the shed door so the people in the house won't see us. "Everyone's looking for you. Are you coming back now? Your mum's dead worried. Dad's calling the police and your gran's probably phoning the Prime Minister by now."

Elin looks so scared I think she's going to cry. Instead she lets out a shaky breath and disentangles herself from the pile of rusty garden stuff she's wrapped up in.

"How did you know I was here?" she asks.

"The werewolves told me which way you'd gone. Well, it turns out they weren't werewolves after all, just a bunch of high-school kids who were hanging about by the bus stop," I told her breathlessly. "I thought they were going to eat me, but they were actually dead nice. They said they'd seen you in the wood and didn't mean to scare you, and you'd run off and hurt yourself. They felt bad about it and—"

"No, I meant, how did you know I was *here*?" Elin interrupts. She's got her robot laser eyes back on but they don't light up any more, like the batteries inside have died or something. It's kind of sad to see.

"You have pictures of this house all over your room. Not that I've been in your room or anything... Well, apart from that one time..." I trail off, embarrassed to remind us both of the destruction I caused. "Anyway, you always look sad when you talk about your old life here. Going past my old house in Southampton used to make me sad too. I know how it feels to—"

"You don't know what it's like to have your perfect family ruined!" Elin snaps. I'm not sure if she's angry because I scared her, or because I wrecked her nice ornaments, or because her little sister's staying at her gran's house. It doesn't really matter why she's mad, cos all that anger's being thrown my way anyhow.

"Your dad hasn't gone and had more kids to replace you, so don't tell me you know how it feels!" She sits down again on her paint tin and buries her head on her arms like she's trying to shut the world out.

"I don't know how it feels," I say sitting down beside her. "I don't know how you're feeling about any of this. I just know how *I* feel. Will I tell you?"

She doesn't tell me to shut up, so I keep talking.

I tell her about all the times I lay awake at night crying because Mum and Dad were shouting at each other downstairs and I was sure it was all my fault.

I tell her about the day Dad left and how it felt like I was losing my best friend in the whole world.

I tell her how I felt about Chris moving in and treating me like I was something nasty he'd got stuck to the bottom of his shoe.

I tell her how I felt when Mum said we were moving to America and I thought I'd never see Dad again.

I tell her how I felt when Mum said I wasn't moving to America and I thought I'd never see her again.

I tell her how scary it was moving to Scotland to a new home with a new stepmum and a stepsister who hated me.

I tell her how hard it's been to make friends in school, and how much the science fair meant to me.

I tell her how finding out she was the one who messed with my medication and wrecked my crystal display made me feel.

Then I tell her what it's like to be different from everyone else, how hard it is to concentrate and control my temper, and how badly I want to be normal.

By the time I finish Elin's crying, but I don't think she's feeling sorry for herself any more. My skin's all sensitive like super-thin tissue paper and I hate being touched, but I hold her hand anyway, and she squeezes it back like it's the only thing holding her together. That's when I realise her other hand is bleeding, and I grab a big piece of tissue I keep in my pocket and set to work wrapping it up.

"It's alright, it's clean," I tell her as she winces in pain. "I always forget to use it and end up wiping my nose on my sleeve anyway."

Elin doesn't look very reassured by that, but she lets me wrap up her hand and tie the ends of the tissue in a little bow. There's a question I want to ask her, but I'm not sure I want to hear the answer. I'm not very good at stopping myself from saying something as soon as it pops into my head though, so it comes rushing out anyway.

"Would you hate me so much if I was normal?" I ask. "Is it because I'm loud and messy and you're quiet and tidy? Is it because—"

"I don't hate you, Jamie," Elin sniffs. "I thought I did. I thought this was all your fault. But you didn't break my family. My mum and dad did."

"My mum and dad broke my family too," I say. "Parents suck."

"Yeah," she nods. It's the first time Elin's ever agreed with anything I've said. It's all the encouragement I need.

"Maybe we should run away together," I suggest. "We could have our own secret runaway club, and live in the park eating Mad Jamie Specials and drinking water from the fountain."

"That's a terrible idea," Elin snorts.

"Why? We'd be free! Wouldn't that be better than fighting all the time?"

"Not if I had to eat your weird sandwiches every day. I'd starve in five minutes. They're horrible!"

"How do you know? You've never tried them. Wait!"

I switch my Transformers torch back on and rummage about in my backpack for the plastic bag I prepared before Dad and Liz hustled me into the car earlier. I take it out and open it up, offering her one of the sticky pieces of bread inside. She pulls a face, but I can tell she's starving cos she picks it up anyway and shoves it in her mouth like she hasn't eaten in a week. In a few seconds flat the big frown on her face turns into a smile.

"Hey! This isn't bad. I could get used to eating these."

"You should've tried them ages ago!" I grin.

"I know," Elin says so quietly I almost don't hear. "It's me that's horrible, not your sandwiches." Her cheeks turn a funny red colour in the torchlight, making her look like an overripe tomato. I'm not an expert, but I think that means she's ashamed.

"If you like them I could make a whole load of them, and we could go on a picnic with your mum and my dad when we get back," I suggest, trying to cheer her up. "Then they'd know we weren't fighting any more and they'd stop arguing and make up and we could all live happily ever after. What do you say?"

Elin thinks for a long minute, and then she says, "Maybe you're like your sandwiches, Jamie – weird and messy and different from anything I'm used to, but not so bad on the inside. Maybe I could get used to you too."

"You think we could start again?" I ask hopefully. "You think we could be a family – you and me and Dad and your mum?"

Elin frowns again and looks at her feet. Forgiveness is hard for her. It's hard for me too, but I throw all the thoughts of her messing with my medication and ruining my science project into a big bin in my head and shut the lid tight.

"I'm sick of fighting, Elin. Can we try to make our family work? Please?"

Elin looks up and gives me a tired nod. She doesn't look happy, but she doesn't look mad any more either. "OK," she says, "I'm sick of this war too."

I smile in the dark, remembering the World War Two project I'd done at my old school. It was like we'd just signed a peace treaty, and we were finally on the same side.

We might not be good friends yet, but for the first time ever, we were allies.

Elin

"I thought when Jamie and me came home together we could all try again," I told Doctor Murray sadly. "But it's too late to fix the mess we made. Everything's broken."

"There are very few things that can't be fixed," she said, leaning forward in her seat and giving me an encouraging smile. "Tell me what it is you think has gone wrong."

I took a deep breath and fiddled with the bandage on my hand. Mum was sending me to see a therapist twice a week now, to deal with my 'anger issues'. It was only my second visit, but Doctor Murray was making me feel better already. It was nice being able to tell someone how I felt without worrying about them being upset or disappointed by what I said.

"Well," I began, "Mum and Paul split up the night I ran away, and now Paul's living in a hotel with Jamie, and Mum cries into her pillow every night when she goes to bed. It's all my fault."

"Why do you think that, Elin?" Doctor Murray asked.

"I thought getting rid of Paul and Jamie was what I wanted.

I thought Mum and Dad would get back together and we'd all live happily ever after."

"And that isn't what you want any more?"

She let the question hang in the air for a bit while I thought about it.

The house was so quiet now without Jamie. It used to annoy me coming home from school to find Paul humming away as he cooked in the kitchen. Now I came home to silence. By the time Mum got home from work, stressed, tired and desperate for a hug, we couldn't seem to find anything to talk about.

I was so lonely I wanted to scream.

"No," I finally shook my head. "It isn't."

Doctor Murray gave me a big smile and scribbled some more notes on her pad.

"Well done Elin, we'll leave it there for today. Will you remember the calming exercises I showed you when you get upset or frustrated by something?"

I nodded and fiddled with my bandage some more while Mum came back in and talked in a hushed voice with Doctor Murray for a bit. My hand was still sore, but the ache I felt when I saw how sad Mum was these days hurt far worse.

When we left the therapist's office and went back to the car Mum gave me a hug and tried to smile.

"Doctor Murray says you're doing really well," she told me. "I'm really proud of you pet, you're trying so hard."

That made me want to cry. I'd been so mean and nasty and ruined everything for her, and she was still acting like I was the best daughter in the whole world. Instead I took deep breaths and imagined a picture of a nice peaceful beach in my head, just like Doctor Murray had told me.

I wonder if this is what Jamie does when he gets upset by something? I thought as we drove home in silence. *Maybe I'll ask him when we—*

Oh.

I couldn't ask him.

He didn't live with us any more.

I helped Mum unpack the shopping and make dinner, and we ate it on the sofa while we watched a film together. Mum used to say that eating dinner off your lap in front of the TV was 'uncivilised', but since Paul and Jamie left we'd been doing it all the time. It was too hard sitting in the kitchen together trying to come up with things to say that didn't upset us both.

Mum went to finish a work report while I did the washing-up. As I wiped down the surfaces, I noticed there was a little package tucked between the bread bin and the fridge. When I pulled it out, I saw it was one of Jamie's jam sandwiches, going mouldy inside its cling film wrapping. He must've left it there the morning I ran away. He'd probably made it specially for me, and I'd paid him back by smashing all his hard work up and stopping him showing everyone how clever he really was.

I couldn't believe I'd been so cruel.

I threw the mouldy sandwich in the bin and headed for my room, finally making up my mind to do something I should've done a whole week ago.

I sat down on my bed, grabbed the cheap phone Dad and Sue bought me at Christmas, and messaged Jamie.

Elin: It's Elin. U OK? When U coming back 2
school?

I waited for a bit, but there was no reply. I sighed and put the phone down, flicking impatiently through a book. Waiting was hard when I couldn't think of anything to do to pass the time. After Jamie's room-wrecking meltdown, I'd had to bin all my broken ornaments, but I didn't feel like painting any replacements. Doctor Murray was right – maybe I was better off without all the reminders of the past cluttering up my room.

My phone pinged and I snatched it up, scrolling through Jamie's message and grinning at how good it made me feel to hear from him again.

Jamie: SO BORED!!! Dad won't let me unpack my
science kit & this rubbish hotel's a dump.
What U doing?

Elin: Nothing. Bored too.

After a long pause, the phone pinged again.

Jamie: Awesome butterfly prog on Discovery in 5
mins. U want 2 watch it with me?

Elin: OK

I typed with one hand as I headed into the living room to turn on the TV. I wasn't that into insects in real life, but when Jamie and Paige had been friends they'd spent most of their time in the playground hunting for bugs, and it had looked like fun. And maybe my science project would've been a bigger success if I'd bothered to learn something about butterflies instead of just painting them.

Elin: When U coming back 2 school?

Jamie: Maybe tmrw. Dad says got to get used to meds again 1st.

There was a big long pause while I thought what to type. When I'd told Mum and Paul what I'd done with Jamie's medication, Paul wasn't mad at me. He was mad at Mum for letting me anywhere near Jamie's capsules, and that was even worse. There was only one thing I could say about what I'd done.

Elin: Sorry. I'm so sorry.

This time the pause was so long the butterfly programme had started by the time the next message came through.

Jamie: It's OK. I feel better now. See U in school tmrw OK? I'll bring U Mad Jamie Specials 4 lunch.

I stared at the message, swallowing hard to get rid of the lump that was forming in my throat. Jamie forgave me. Jamie *always* forgave me. I'd been wrong about the war. Jamie had been on my side right from the start.

I hit a button and sent him the one thing he'd wanted from me since he turned up on our doorstep all those months ago.

I sent him a smiley face.

Elin:

40

Jamie

"… And glasswing butterflies are the most amazing thing ever," I explain, stuffing more jam sandwich in my face and forgetting Elin hates it when I talk with my mouth full. "Their wings are transparent, so you can see right through them!"

Elin doesn't tell me off. She grins back and eats her Mad Jamie Specials like they're the most amazing thing ever too. I wish she'd tried them the first night I came to stay at her house. Then maybe we could've been friends right from the start. I miss Paige so much it hurts, but sitting with Elin at lunch is almost as good.

"You two still not speaking?" Elin glances across to where Paige is sitting on her own at another table. Elin's good at reading people. She knows what I'm thinking without me telling her. It's kind of spooky, but it's also kind of awesome. I don't have her superpower though. I don't know what Elin's thinking, so I have to guess. Elin's never liked Paige, so she probably wants to make sure I won't hang about with her any more.

"No," I shrug, pretending I don't care. "I said some bad things when I was off my medication, and now I think she's scared of me."

"Oh," Elin says.

I don't know what that means either, so I say, "You want to come bug hunting with me at break? Dad got me a new tank at the weekend. I'm going to build my own caterpillar army and take over the world. You want to help and be Queen Elin of the butterfly people?"

Elin laughs at that, and I'm glad I can make her smile now. But then she looks serious again and says, "Are you allowed to keep bugs in your hotel room? Aren't there rules against it?"

"We're not staying much longer. Dad's got a friend who's going away to Spain on business for a couple of months. He's going to let Dad rent his house till Dad decides if we're staying here or moving back to Southampton in the summer holidays."

"Oh," Elin says again.

I wish she'd stop saying that. I'm about to ask her if she'd be sad if I moved away, but just then the lunch monitor comes sneaking up with a big mean grin on her face.

"Did you have another meltdown, Freak-Boy?" Rachel sneers at me. "What's wrong, is the school milk not as good as the stuff they served at the loony bin you were locked up in last week?"

She's pointing to the mess under the table a couple of seats down from me. Darren got up in a hurry to go and play football, and knocked over his carton of milkshake. There's pink goo running off the end of the table and making a big messy puddle on the floor, and Rachel's trying to pin the blame on me. Miss Morrison's buying her own lunch at the canteen hatch just now. If I'm not careful she'll come marching over and tell me to go to her lunchtime homework club. I can't risk that today. Mr Jones the PE teacher's only just let me back on the football team, and I need to go to the lunchtime practice or he'll give my place to someone else.

"I wasn't in a loony bin," I say very slowly and carefully. "I was at home with Dad. I didn't spill the milkshake, you know I didn't. You saw Darren knock it over."

I can feel the hairs on the back of my neck prickling and my face getting hot. Rachel knows exactly which buttons to press. She's an expert at overloading my systems and making me blow up.

"I don't care if you were in a loony bin or in prison for setting fire to your own farts," Rachel says. "Get that mess cleaned up or I'm telling Miss Morrison you're throwing milkshake bombs at the other kids."

"That's not fair!" I yell, my hands clenching into fists and my voice going all high-pitched and squeaky. "Elin, tell her it isn't fair, that's not my milk!"

Elin doesn't say anything though. She's sitting opposite me, but she might as well be on another planet for all the support I get from her. She doesn't even look up, she just keeps right on eating and reading the back of her crisp packet like it's the world's most interesting gossip magazine.

That makes me almost as mad as Rachel's non-stop meanness. At least Paige used to stand up for me, even if nobody listened to her.

"I know it's not yours," Rachel laughs nastily, "but I'm going to make sure you get the blame for it anyway. Who's Miss Morrison going to believe – me, or a total mental case like you?"

"She'll make me go to the homework club!" I'm almost crying

now with the effort not to explode into a million pieces. "I'll lose my place on the football team!"

"Good!" Rachel's grin gets even wider, and I can't take any more.

"I hate you!" I yell at the top of my voice, throwing a sandwich right in her face.

"Jamie Lee! Stop that right now!" Miss Morrison roars so loud across the canteen it sounds like she's got a microphone sellotaped to her mouth. "What's going on?"

Before I can get my breath back, Rachel's already telling lies about me throwing milkshake and calling her nasty names and bullying her, and Miss Morrison's got her hands on her hips and is saying the dreaded words: 'homework club'.

"She's LYING!" I yell, my whole head fizzing with rage. "Why doesn't anyone ever believe me? She's the one who's bullying *me*!"

"Jamie, you're the liar," Mrs Morrison snaps, cutting me off. "Now go to the janitor and get a mop to clean your mess up before I make it two days at the homework club instead of one."

"IT'S NOT FAIR!"

The last thing I see before the red mist of uncontrollable rage descends and I run away is Elin watching me with a big smile on her face.

She isn't on my side like she said. She doesn't want her mum and my dad to get back together so I can come and live with her again. She hasn't ended the war and signed the peace treaty after all.

She was just pretending.

41

Elin

It was hard to admit it, but I owed Jamie big time. When he came to live with us I'd thought he was a monster who was keeping my family apart, but he turned out to be a knight in food-stained armour who had a Transformers torch instead of a sword. If I ever wrote my story again, then Jamie would be the Knight who rescued the Perfect Princess from the werewolves in the Tangled Wood and helped her escape from the Pit of Despair.

Jamie didn't tell the teachers that I was the one who ruined his science display, and he wouldn't let his dad talk to Miss Morrison about it either. He could've made the whole world see how bad I really was, and he chose not to.

He was a way better person than I'd ever be.

None of the teachers knew that though. They all thought I was perfect and Jamie was a monster. Miss Morrison even believed the nasty lies Rachel told about Jamie.

I was pretty sure Paul was so stressed that today's drama might be the final straw that sent him packing to Southampton with

Jamie, and I'd never see either of them again.

All I had to do was keep my mouth shut and I'd get the very thing I'd been desperate for six months ago.

But Doctor Murray had helped me see that wasn't what I wanted.

What I wanted now was to try to make family life with Jamie and Paul work. It wouldn't be easy – it would mean being braver in real life than the Perfect Princess had ever been in my story. But it was time for me to stop making up fairy tales and tell the truth to Mum and my teachers.

It was time to learn from Jamie and do something good for a change.

When the home-time bell rang I didn't even say goodbye to Jamie, I just grabbed my schoolbag and ran out to the car park. Mum was meeting me after school so we could go shopping for a new computer to replace the one Jamie had beaten to death with my wardrobe door. She said we needed to do something nice together to try to 'get things back to normal'.

"Are you ready to go shopping?" Mum asked when I opened the car door.

"Not yet," I told her. "There's something we need to do first."

I grabbed her arm and led her back into school, going so fast we nearly bumped right into Paul and Jamie outside the head teacher's office.

"Liz! What are you doing here? Did the school call you too?" Paul looked even more confused than Mum did.

"No… I didn't know you were here. Elin, what's this about?

You said you wanted to talk to the head teacher?"

They all turned to stare at me. It was now or never. I took a deep breath and opened Mr Conway's door. Miss Morrison was sitting in there too, her frown making Jamie shrink down into his jacket when we walked in.

Before the adults could say a single word, I blurted out, "Miss Morrison, Jamie's been telling the truth all this time – Rachel's the one who's been bullying him and trying to get him to lose his temper. She says mean things to him every day and winds him up in class when you're not looking."

I could hear a little gasp of surprise from somewhere inside the hood Jamie was hiding beneath.

"I'm well aware that Rachel Young isn't perfect, Elin," Miss Morrison said, "but Jamie certainly isn't innocent. He—"

"But he IS innocent!" I insisted, interrupting our teacher and making her gasp in surprise too. "He's never once started it – all those times you asked what happened and I said it was Jamie, I was lying. I've been helping get him into trouble too. I knew you'd believe me and not him, that's why at the science fair competition..."

It was hard to get the words out, and I had to take another deep breath before I could finish.

"What I mean is, Jamie didn't ruin his science fair entry. *I* did," I finally managed to admit. "Jamie was telling the truth when he said it wasn't him, and he's been telling the truth about Rachel. Here, I can prove it."

Before Mr Conway could open his mouth, I pulled my phone from my pocket and pressed play on a video. Rachel's voice filled the room, and a moment later Jamie's joined in.

"*Did you have another meltdown, Freak-Boy? What's wrong, is the school milk not as good as they stuff they served at the loony bin you were locked up in last week?*"

Everyone watched wide-eyed as Rachel insulted Jamie, and Miss Morrison's mouth was hanging open in amazement by the time we got to the end of the argument.

"*She'll make me go to the homework club! I'll lose my place on the football team!*"

"*Good!*"

I pressed pause on the video, and the whole screen filled with Rachel's sneering face. Miss Morrison blinked hard. Mr Conway cleared his throat awkwardly. Mum and Paul exchanged glances and Jamie stood there grinning under his hood.

He'd finally realised I hadn't been ignoring him and reading my crisp packet while Rachel was winding him up.

I'd been recording them.

The next few minutes passed in a blur. Miss Morrison and Mr Conway didn't shout, but they did say a lot of stern words that made my eyes blur with tears and my fists clench to stop them falling. Mum took my hand and gave it a squeeze when they'd finished telling me off, and knowing she was proud of me for doing the right thing made me choke up even more. I was too upset to hear what Miss Morrison and Mr Conway said about punishing Rachel, but it made Jamie happy, as his grin got even wider.

After it was over, we walked back out to the car park in silence. No one knew what to say. Mum and Paul looked like a couple of teenagers on their first date, and Jamie was skipping round and round like a kangaroo who'd just won the Australian lottery.

I was too dazed to feel awkward though. I had to go to the lunchtime homework club every day for a month and Miss Morrison had said the dreaded word: 'disappointed'.

The thing that I'd been most afraid of ever since Dad left had finally happened. Everyone had found out I wasn't the Perfect Princess and that I'd done terrible things.

And you know what the really strange thing was? The world hadn't ended.

I did feel pretty awful, but I also felt lighter somehow, like I imagined the sky felt after a storm when the thunder rolled away and the clouds finally parted.

We stopped by Mum's car, and she rummaged about in her handbag for ages pretending to look for her keys. We both knew they were in her pocket. She just wanted a chance to talk to Paul. He was clearly looking for an opportunity too. Instead of driving straight off with Jamie, he hung around pretending to examine the worn tyres on Mum's car and telling her she should get them changed.

I knew I should do something to help them get back together. I was the one who broke this family, so it was my job to fix it again. I just wasn't sure how.

"That was a brave thing you did in there, Elin, I'm proud of you," Paul said when he'd run out of imaginary problems with Mum's car. "Thanks for sticking up for Jamie and telling the truth."

I shrugged and nodded, then I looked away. I wanted to tell him I was sorry for all the mean things I'd said to him since he came to live with me and Mum, and that I missed him. I missed the sound of him cooking in the kitchen and the nights we spent making popcorn and watching films I pretended to hate. I missed playing board games and having family time in the evenings, and I even missed him asking me lots of questions about school that I hardly ever answered. I couldn't say any of that though. There was a lump in my throat the size of an apple and I couldn't choke it down.

"Are you coming then, Elin? It's time to go." Mum finally ran out of places to hunt for her car keys and pulled them from her pocket.

"Wait!" I found my voice again just in time. I had to fix this. I just had to. "I can wait till the weekend to get a new computer."

"But I left work early specially so we could go to shops and—"

"I know, but… what if Paul and Jamie came for dinner tonight instead?"

I held my breath. Mum and Paul exchanged hopeful glances.

"You're more than welcome," Mum said quickly. "I made a pot of chilli last night."

"That sounds great, but I thought…" Paul looked back at me, and I could see the doubt in his eyes. "Are you sure, Elin? Are you sure you want me and Jamie there?"

My throat was too tight to give him the answer he was looking for, so instead I gave him something even better, something I'd never given him before.

I gave him a hug.

42

Jamie

Everyone's hugging.

I don't know if I'm supposed to join in, but I don't like hugging, so I just drum my fingers on the bonnet of Liz's car instead till everyone looks round to see what the weird noise is.

"So… does this mean you're getting back together and I can move back into my bedroom again?" I ask Liz. I don't know if she's forgiven me yet for all the trouble I've caused, and the way she looks at the ground and shuffles her feet isn't giving me any clues. Dad takes it as a good sign though, and he whispers something in her ear that makes her smile.

"Let's take one day at a time, OK Sandwich Man?" he says to me.

I'm back to being Sandwich Man again.

This is very definitely a good sign.

They are *so* getting back together.

"Thanks for sticking up for me," I tell Elin. "I'm sorry you have to go to the homework club."

"I'm sorry I wrecked your science project," Elin says. She still looks a bit sad, but I'm pretty sure I can cheer her up with a couple of Mad Jamie Specials when we get home – they can cure just about anything. I don't need to say I'm sorry for breaking all the things in her room.

We're even now.

My medication's worn off and now I'm starving and I want my chilli. I don't want to stand around in the school car park watching people hug. I'm just about to run to Dad's car when he calls me back.

"Hey! Wait a minute, Jamie. I've just remembered something I meant to tell you. There was a notice on the library website the other week – they're running a special science fair entry contest after the Easter holidays for groups. Maybe you and Elin should do a joint project and see if it wins a place. You'd be on the same team for once. What do you think?"

It feels like he's just zapped me with a million volts of electricity. My whole spine's tingling and my hands are shaking with excitement. There's nothing I want more than another shot at that science fair! If I win, I can prove to everyone there's something I'm actually good at. And after the brave thing Elin did for me today, I'm desperate to find a way to pay her back. I know riding lessons are something that would make her really happy.

Elin deserves to be happy. She's been sad for too long.

I bite my lip and grin at her, willing her to say yes.

She frowns in that super-annoying way that's impossible to read, then says, "Maybe. I'll think about it."

It's not as good as a 'yes', but it's close.

"Yes!" I yell for both of us. "Glasgow Science Centre here we come!"

"Not so fast!" Dad laughs. "You haven't even entered yet!"

"Or thought up a project," Liz adds.

"What about your crystals project?" Elin says. "Could we redo it?"

"Nah," I shake my head. "The whole point of science is investigating something you don't already know the answer to. I know everything there is to know about crystals now. Almost."

"Then what could we investigate?"

I've already worked out the answer to that one. I put my hand in my schoolbag and pull out the book I've been carrying about with me ever since Paige gave it to me at Christmas. "We'll study the most amazing thing on the whole planet!" I grin. "BUTTERFLIES!"

Elin can't help smiling back.

I'm going to take that as a 'yes' too.

43

Elin

Our science project was brilliant, but me and Jamie didn't work. There was something missing, some important glue we needed to hold our team together. I was too neat and careful, and Jamie was too messy and excitable. We needed a third team member, but not someone who would try to take over or tell us what to do.

What we needed was a referee.

"There's a girl from school coming round this afternoon," I told Gran as I sorted a pile of leaves onto different plates. "She's going to help us with the science fair entry."

"I'll make some extra hotdogs for lunch," Gran smiled, and I smiled back. Things had been awkward between us after I ran off to her house and found Beth there, but they were getting back to normal again. I was still upset at Gran for lying to me about never seeing Dad's new family, but I was starting to understand why she did it. I would've gone crazy if she'd told me, and I could do a pretty good monster impression myself when I was upset.

"Who's coming for lunch? Who's doing our project with us?" Jamie came stumbling in lugging a big box filled with more leaves to sort. The different caterpillars in our plastic tanks only ate one type of leaf, and we had to be careful to feed them the right ones.

"Don't worry Jamie, it's—"

"You invited someone to be on our science team and you didn't even ask me?" Jamie cried, dropping half the contents of his box on the floor in outrage. "Mrs Watts! Tell her she can't do that!"

"It's OK, we'll just try it for this afternoon and if it doesn't work we'll go back to doing it ourselves," I said quickly, before Gran could leap to Jamie's defence.

Gran had been looking after us for the holidays while Mum and Paul were at work, and now she'd got to know Jamie better she'd been treating him like the grandson she never knew she had. If it wasn't for the fact that he drove her up the wall almost as much as he made her smile then I'd probably be jealous.

"Oh, before you go Elin, there's something I wanted to ask you," Gran said before I could follow Jamie into the garden. I waited, getting a bit nervous when she didn't say it straight away.

"I know you're still upset about your father having another child…"

Here it comes, I thought.

"… but Beth is your sister, and you two would get on so well if you'd just give her a chance. She's desperate to meet you."

I didn't say anything. I just fiddled with the leaf I was holding, ripping it into little bits.

"The thing is…" Gran went on slowly, "your father's starting work again next week, and he needs me to look after Beth until he can arrange a babysitter."

The bits of torn leaf were piling up on the plate now, but I still didn't say anything.

"Do you see the problem?" Gran asked, trying to get me to help her out. I knew what she wanted me to say, but I wanted her to spell it out for me first. Maybe if I stalled for long enough I wouldn't have to make the big decision I knew was coming.

Gran sighed and came straight out with it. "Your mother needs me to look after you and Jamie this Easter, and your father needs me to babysit Beth. I can do both, but I can't be in two places at once. Would you mind if I brought her here? Honestly Elin, I think you'd love her to bits if you'd just agree to spend some time with her."

I dropped the last ripped leaf onto a plate and wiped my hands slowly on a paper towel before I answered. "Let me think about it, OK Gran?" It was the best I could do. Gran knew I was trying, so she gave me a hug and left it at that.

"Elin, are you bringing those leaves or what?" Jamie yelled from the back garden.

"Hang on!" I called back. "I'm going to get another notebook." We already had a huge pile of stationery for recording our results, but I needed a minute to process what Gran had just said. I went to my room and opened my desk drawer, but I wasn't looking for paper. It was the folder hiding beneath my photo albums I was after.

I opened it up, flicking through the pages inside and staring at all the chapters of the story I'd written since Mum and Dad split up. It was all lies. If I'd just been prepared to give Beth and Sue a chance like Gran said, I could've seen Dad as much as I wanted, and I wouldn't have had to make up all my stupid fairy tales about my old family getting back together.

It was time to write a new story. A real story, with real characters instead of made-up ones.

I closed the folder of lies and shoved it back in my drawer.

"OK Gran," I said as I headed out to join Jamie in the back garden, "you can bring Beth here next week."

Gran's smile was so wide I knew I'd just made her prouder of me than the Perfect Princess could ever have done.

44

Jamie

"Photo time!" I announce, grabbing my phone and pulling my two team members into the picture. I want to prove to Mum that she doesn't need to worry about me any more, and make her proud of me so she can enjoy her American Dream Life. And maybe I want to make Chris feel just a little bit jealous that he doesn't have a super-awesome butterfly experiment in his back garden too.

"Not again, Jamie!" Elin sighs. "We still have to measure each caterpillar and draw up the size-comparison charts. We don't have time for more pictures."

"We've still got all day tomorrow," Paige says, taking her glasses off and smiling at the camera, "and there's only two more charts to do, so there's plenty of time."

Paige is a lot less shy than she was when she knocked on our door a week ago holding an old school jotter for science notes and half a bag of Liquorice Allsorts to bribe Elin to be nice to her. She didn't need to bribe me. I was desperate to be her friend again. It took a few days for Elin to stop ordering her around and for Paige to stop looking like a mouse stuck to the tarmac on the motorway, but it's going great now. Paige knows exactly how to calm me down when I start getting angry and frustrated, and I haven't blown up in two whole days. She's like a bomb-disposal expert who knows just where to cut the fuse before there's an explosion, and she's helping Elin get along better with me too.

The weather's been perfect here all Easter, probably even better than sunny California. I stretch out on the grass and take another selfie with my magnifying glass up to my eye like I'm a famous bug hunter. Miss Morrison told me on the last day of term that I was smart enough to be a scientist when I leave school. She's never said anything like that to me before. I think that was her way of apologising for not believing me about Rachel and for shouting at me for all sorts of things that weren't my fault.

She doesn't need to worry about that. I've still got plenty of Mad Jamie meltdowns left in me to keep her yelling at me till the end of June.

At least Dad and Liz aren't yelling at each other any more. I've been on my very best behaviour, which usually isn't enough, but this time round it's like we're all working together instead of taking sides in a war against each other. Our family's not perfect, but for the first time in ages, I'm starting to think just maybe it might stay together for good this time.

"Lunchtime!" Mrs Watts calls from the kitchen. "You three need to take a break for a little while and come and have something to eat."

We all pile into the kitchen to drink orange juice and eat hotdogs. I'm not that hungry because of my medication, but

Mrs Watts has made them specially cos she thinks they're my favourite thing just now. I don't want to tell her I actually like beans on toast way better, so I chew on one anyway and look at the pictures Beth's been painting in here while we worked on our experiment.

"Hey! I like this one. Is it a tortoiseshell?" I ask, holding up the butterfly-shaped paper with black and orange blobs covering it.

"Don't be daft," Elin rolls her eyes at me, "it's a painted lady. Can't you see the wing markings? It's very accurate for a three year old."

"Ack-u-late," Beth agrees, grinning at Elin and popping another fistful of hotdog sausage in her mouth.

Elin's got a new project now that she likes even better than painting all her little fairy-tale figures, and that's teaching Beth how to paint. I thought she'd insist on doing all our science display artwork herself, but she's letting Beth help. It's nice seeing the two of them getting along, even if it does mean some of our information posters are going to be a bit wonky. It makes me feel hopeful seeing the blobby butterflies going into our display box. If Elin's changed from a control freak into a patient big sister who doesn't mind a bit of mess, it means there's hope that I've changed from a monster into something much better too.

"Do you think we can win the science fair?" Paige asks me for about the zillionth time. "I've never won anything in my life."

"Of course we can win," Elin says, wiping Beth's fingers and showing her how to open her yoghurt. "Our project's brilliant."

Mrs Watts frowns, and I know she's worrying about Elin being overconfident and how we still have to get our display past the judges at the library next week before we can think about making it to the Glasgow Science Centre. I'm not worried though. I've got the best reason in the world for wanting to win, and I can't wait to see Elin's face when we're handed first prize and I tell her she'll be able to get her riding lessons at last.

I already feel like a winner. Elin and I joined forces in the war and won a proper family as a prize. That's almost better than winning all the science competitions on the planet.

Elin

Winning a place at the science fair in the library competition a few weeks ago was the easy part.

On the day of the fair it wasn't the judges walking round the crowded Science Centre with their clipboards that made me nervous. It was seeing Dad together with his new family for the very first time that made my heart flutter faster than the newly emerged butterflies in our tanks.

"Do you see him?" I asked yet again, craning my neck to look for his familiar blond hair in the crowd. There were lots of kids from our school here, and Miss Morrison had come over to say hello, but I hadn't seen any sign of Dad and he hadn't called. "He said he'd come. Do you think he's changed his mind?"

"Don't worry, he'll be here. He wouldn't miss this for the world." Mum squeezed my hand and gave me a reassuring smile that helped a bit, but I couldn't stop worrying about what I'd say to Sue when I saw her. She'd been trying for over three years to get me to accept her, inviting me to spend holidays in Edinburgh and sending little presents along with Dad whenever I saw him at Gran's house, but I rejected her every time. I was scared it was too late and I'd wrecked my chance to give my story a different ending.

"Ow! That was my foot!" I yelped, getting out of the way before Jamie could crush my toes again. "Stop bouncing up and down! If you need the toilet just go, the judges still have three more tables to look at before it's our turn."

"Don't-need-to-pee," Jamie said, all wound up with twitchy energy. "Just-nervous. Forgot-my-chewing-gum."

"Here, I brought some for you." Paige pulled a couple of packs from her pocket and handed them to him, and I fought the sudden urge to hug her. She was *so* good at this. A few months ago I thought she was rubbish at everything, but now I knew that wasn't true.

She'd make a great teacher one day. She was way more patient than I'd ever be.

"Hey, look!" Jamie said through a mouthful of gum. "There's Beth!"

He didn't need to point her out. As soon as she saw us Beth let go of Dad's hand and came running straight for me, throwing herself at my knees and demanding to be picked up and hugged. She was so like me it made me smile. Once she'd decided someone was family, she'd hold on tight and never let go.

As I showed Beth the butterflies in the tanks, I tried not to notice that Dad was holding Sue's hand and Paul had his arm around Mum's waist. They weren't putting on a show for each other though. They all looked happy and relaxed for the first time ever, and Gran was smiling so much at all of them I was worried her face was going to crack.

Then Sue came over and pretended to wipe Beth's nose, but I knew she was just looking for an excuse to talk to me.

"Hi Elin, it's lovely to meet you at last. Your dad's told me so much about you I feel like I know you already."

"Um, yeah, nice to meet you too," I stammered. I wasn't sure if that was true, but it was such a relief to let go of all the anger I'd been carrying around that I felt about ten tons lighter.

"How about I take some pictures of you three with your science display? Your gran would love one to put on her wall, and I told all my friends at work I'd bring in photos of your experiments to show them. Just there's perfect. Say cheese!"

Jamie grimaced when I put my arm round his shoulder and Paige leaned in close, but my smile was real. Sue was still trying to make friends with me, and that meant I hadn't blown my chance to spend holiday time with Dad and Beth in Edinburgh after all.

That made me feel even better than winning this place at the science fair.

"Look, the judges are coming," Paul said suddenly, and my stomach did another nervous somersault. "Good luck guys, we've got our fingers crossed for you."

They all stepped back so the judges could look at our display and ask us questions.

The moment we'd been working towards for all these weeks had finally arrived.

I was so nervous I could barely answer the judges' questions, and I kept tripping over my words and stammering. I was desperate to do well and make Dad proud of me, but the fear of letting everyone down tangled up my tongue until I couldn't speak. Jamie didn't do much better – he garbled his answers so fast as he bounced up and down like a jack-in-the-box that the judges had no hope of understanding a single word he said.

It was Paige who got us through it.

She was nervous too, but somehow she managed to hold herself together and speak slowly and clearly, telling the judges all about our experiment design and the different stages of our butterflies' growth. She was so much braver when she wasn't being bullied by Rachel, or frowned at by Miss Morrison.

Or treated really badly by me.

As soon as the judges finished writing on their clipboards and moved on to the next entry, Jamie let out a long breath that sounded like a balloon deflating, and I grabbed Paige's hand and gave it a squeeze.

"You were *brilliant!*" I whispered.

Paige grinned back at me and blushed, and it felt like all the times I'd said mean things to her or just ignored her when she wanted to talk to me in school had finally been forgiven.

The rest of the afternoon passed in a blur. In no time at all the moment we'd all been waiting for arrived, and everyone gathered back in the main hall to hear the judges announce the runners-up and winners.

"Do you think we'll win?" Jamie kept whispering in my ear so loud the whole hall could hear him. "Do you think we will?"

"I don't know!" I whispered back. "Just stand still for half a second and we'll find out!"

I tried to convince myself I didn't care about the result. I told myself that by putting all our differences aside and working together we'd already won a prize way better than the thousand pounds. I said all the right things in my head, but it still didn't stop my stomach from lurching in disappointment when the results were announced.

We didn't win the science fair.

Our entry came second.

I could hear Paige's squeal of delight being drowned out by Jamie's half-strangled howl of outrage, and I had to almost drag him up to the stage with us so he could collect his certificate. He managed to keep a smile on his face for the whole time it took to dismantle our display and get it packed up again into Mum's car, but I knew it was fake.

While the adults stood chatting in the car park, Jamie pretended he was checking we'd stowed everything away, but he was really hiding behind the boot so no one would see he was trying hard not to cry. It wasn't the perfect ending I'd been hoping for either, but seeing him so sad made me realise there were some things more important than winning.

"Cheer up," I whispered, "we did so well. We came second in the whole of Glasgow! Our experiment was really good."

"Not good enough to win the thousand pounds," Jamie sniffed.

"We still get fifty pounds each. That's not bad, is it?"

"Yeah, but it won't be *enough*."

"Enough for what?" I asked, confused. Jamie hadn't mentioned the prize money before. I thought he just wanted to win to prove to everyone he was good at science.

"For *riding lessons*," he said, wiping his nose on his sleeve. "If I can't pay for them, then I can't make up for ruining everything for you when I came to stay."

I could only stand there and blink at him in amazement.

"You mean all this time you've been trying to win just so I can go riding?" I finally asked.

He nodded, staring at his feet.

"Jamie, if you didn't hate it so much, I'd hug you right now," I laughed.

"You mean you're not disappointed?"

"Dad's gone back to work, so he's going to pay for me to start riding lessons next month. The only thing I'm disappointed in is myself. I've been really mean to you, and you've been so nice to me," I admitted. "I wish I could go back in time and undo all the bad things I've done."

It was Jamie's turn to stare at me in surprise. Then his frown turned into a big grin.

"If I didn't hate hugging so much, I'd hug you right now too," he smiled. That made us both laugh.

"There you are!" Dad said, finding our hiding place. "Elin, we're heading over to your gran's house now. Do you need a lift somewhere, Paige? Or is your mum coming to pick you up?"

I felt a sudden stab of guilt. I'd been so focused on Jamie I'd forgotten all about Paige sitting quietly on the wall by herself. I got the feeling she was used to that happening.

"It's OK," she said. "I can get the bus back."

She glanced over at me then looked away quickly, fiddling with the sleeves of her baggy jumper. It took me a minute to realise she wasn't just embarrassed that her mum had to work today and she had no one else to come and cheer her on at the science fair. She was disappointed too. She thought now the science fair was over she didn't matter to me any more and I was going to go back to ignoring her again.

"Why don't you come with us to Whitburn?" I asked. "We're going to have a picnic tea in my gran's garden. We can call your mum and ask if it's OK, but I'm sure she won't mind."

Paige didn't say anything, but she nodded so hard her glasses nearly fell off.

I wasn't sure if we'd ever be best friends, just like I wasn't sure if I'd ever be totally happy about Mum and Dad being with different people. But I'd got used to having Jamie as a brother and I was starting to like having Beth as a little sister, so I was willing to give Paige a try too.

Everyone piled into the cars, but Dad gave me a hug before I got in beside Jamie and Paige.

"You did so well today, pet," he smiled. "I'm so proud of you."

Dad wasn't talking about the science fair. He was talking about me giving Sue and Beth a chance. Ever since he left I'd been tying myself up in knots trying to prove to him how perfect I was so he'd come back and be my dad again. It had taken Jamie turning my family inside out before I realised Dad had never left me, and all I had to do to get him back in my life was to stop making the people he cared about into fairy-tale monsters.

I'd got it wrong for so long. I thought being perfect meant sucking up to teachers and sticking to the rules no matter who I hurt along the way. I was so busy trying to look good on the outside I didn't realise how ugly I was on the inside. I didn't need to be perfect.

All I had to be was kind, just like Paige.

"I'm *starving*!" Jamie announced. "If we don't get to Whitburn for our food *right now* I'm going to start eating our science experiment."

"We'd better get going then," Dad laughed, waving to Mum and Paul and heading off to Sue's car.

"I wish we didn't have to drive there, I wish we could just teleport. If I had a time machine and a teleporter I could… Hey! Elin! Paige! I've got a BRILLIANT idea for our next science experiment!"

"Not another one!" I rolled my eyes, but I jumped into the back seat beside him, eager to find out what he was going to come up with this time.

Life with Jamie was never going to be easy, but it was turning into an adventure story better than any I'd written before.

46

Jamie

"I *told* you we should've used my Mad Jamie Specials for the final part of the experiment instead of flowers!" I tell my science team. "Look! They totally love them."

"They're not eating them," Elin says, "they're flying away from them. Look at that one – he's trying to drown himself in your cola puddle just to escape your yukky food."

Elin picks the butterfly up on her finger and puts it on a dry patch of grass, but she can only do it with one hand cos she's holding one of my sandwiches in the other.

"You totally love them," I laugh.

"Do not," Elin says, taking another big bite.

Paige gives me a sideways grin, and I snort more cola over my T-shirt trying to swallow my giggles. She goes to show Beth the video she's taken on my phone of me releasing the butterflies, and I stretch out on the grass, staring up at the blue sky and smiling to myself. I'm going to send that video to Mum when we get home. I want to prove to her that I can look after tanks full of caterpillars for weeks and not have them end up living in my bedroom carpet. That'll make her even more proud than my science fair certificate.

"You shouldn't call them that," Elin says. I'm not a mind reader, so I've got no idea what she's talking about.

"What?" I roll over to look at her, trying not to squash any of the butterflies that are fluttering about her gran's back garden.

"Mad Jamie Specials. It's not a nice name. You're not mad, you're just… different."

"Yeah," I sigh, "I'm a total fruit loop." I tap my finger on the side of my head and cross my eyes. My funny face doesn't make her smile though, she just frowns harder.

"But you're not, Jamie, I know that now! I thought I was so perfect, but that's just because I was hiding all my anger inside instead of letting it out like you. Doctor Murray's made me see that. Everyone finds life a bit hard to deal with sometimes. If everyone who struggled with difficult things was mad, then that'd mean the whole world was insane. It's OK to be different, and not do things the same way as everyone else."

"Does this mean I get a free pass next time I throw a wobbly at the dinner table?" I grin at her.

"As long as we don't have to eat your favourite food for five nights in a row you can do what you like." Elin's frown turns into a grimace.

"So what do you think my sandwiches should be called then?" I ask.

"What about 'Sandwich Man Specials'? That's what your dad calls them."

"Sandwich Man Specials…" I think for a bit. "Yeah, I like that!"

Elin finally smiles back at me and pops the last of her sandwich in her mouth.

"Ten more minutes guys, then we're going home," Dad calls from the kitchen, where the grown-ups have been sitting round the table drinking coffee. "Make sure all of the butterflies are out of those tanks before you take them back to the car."

I throw him a salute, and he grins back. I know he's prouder of me today than he's ever been in my whole life, and that makes me so happy I feel like dancing.

"Jamie, do you want to help me with something?" Elin asks before I start tap dancing across the grass. "There's something I need to get rid of."

She takes a big folder out of her backpack and carries it over to the barbecue that's still smoking on the patio. The flames have gone out after our dinner, but the coals are still glowing red-hot.

"Here. Scrunch these up and burn them. Don't read them, OK? And be careful this time!" Elin says, pulling some pages from the folder and making them into a little paper ball that she dumps on the coals. They shrivel up and disappear in a cloud of ash, and it looks like so much fun I'm already making my own balls to burn before it even occurs to me to ask what we're doing.

Suddenly I catch sight of the words 'Princess' and 'Monster' as some of the paper turns black, and I finally figure out what we're burning. "Are these all of your stories?" I gasp. "Elin! Why are you destroying them?"

"I should've done it a long time ago," Elin says, dumping more pages on the growing pile of hot ash. "They were making me sad." She doesn't look sad now though, just sort of strong and

251

determined. It's a much better look than the laser-eyed robot or the creepy china-doll face she used to wear.

I'm pretty sure I can work out who 'the Princess' and 'the Monster' are, but there's one name I can't stop myself from asking about. "Who's 'the Slug'?"

"Hey! I told you not to read them!"

"I couldn't help it! I just saw it for a moment before it burned. Is that what you called Rachel from school?"

Elin shakes her head. "It was… someone I was wrong about. Someone I should've called 'the Caterpillar'."

"Why? Did they like eating leaves?" I ask.

"No, because at the end of the story they turned out to be a beautiful butterfly."

Elin won't say any more than that, but her eyes dart to where Paige is sitting with Beth on her knee, showing her the videos on my phone. They're both giggling so hard it makes me smile too.

"You're not still sad we didn't win, are you?" she asks, tidying up the picnic blanket and putting the empty folder back in her bag. "Coming second was a really big achievement."

"Yeah, we've done well," I nod, but I'm not really thinking about the science fair. Elin and me have come so far these last few months it's like we've been running the world's hardest marathon and we're almost at the finish line.

The best thing is we're all friends now, and we're running this last bit together. Not everything's about being perfect and winning first place.

"Come on guys, time to go home," Dad calls again. "Jamie, don't forget the tanks."

Beth jumps off Paige's knee and runs to take Elin's hand, and Elin feeds her the last of the sandwiches when she thinks I'm not looking.

"That was an amazing day," Paige sighs. "I wish we could do a science fair every weekend."

"I bet there're more competitions we can enter," Elin agrees, "let's look online when we get back. Do you want to come over to ours for a bit? It's not late yet. Your mum won't mind, will she? Maybe she'd let you sleep over. We could watch films and eat ice cream and popcorn."

"And more of your sandwiches?" Paige asks me hopefully.

I grin at them. "Sounds like the best plan ever. Race you back to the car. Last one there has to clean up the mess I make!"

We all start running down the garden, but I'm carrying the biggest tank so I can't catch them. I don't mind though. Everyone looks happy tonight, and that's all I care about. I've got a family that accepts me for who I am, and that makes me smile even when I lose.

Life with me is never going to be perfect, but I'm doing my best. I know now I'm not broken, and I don't need fixed. I might be different, and seem a bit weird at first, like jam and cream and peanut butter all mixed up together. But everyone loves my Sandwich Man Specials when they're willing to give them a try.

And maybe, if people give me a chance, they'll find they like me just as much too.

Acknowledgements

My exciting writing journey would not have been possible without the amazing support of my mother and brother Martin, who have not only joined me over the years on my literary adventures, but have provided a safe haven and support when the seas turned stormy and the going got rough. I've been very lucky to have also had the support of friends and family who, I hope, all know how much I appreciate their encouragement.

My agent Ben Illis deserves a medal for the time, patience and care he devotes to each and every one of his authors, and I can't thank him enough for all of his hard work on my behalf.

Thanks also to my two very talented editors, Sally Polson and Jennie Skinner, who have helped shape Elin and Jamie's story with all of their insightful suggestions and ideas. Under their guidance, *The Boy with the Butterfly Mind* has evolved into a more nuanced and well-rounded novel.

Finally, I'd like to thank Scottish charity Children 1st for collaborating on the book launch and for reviewing the novel before publication to ensure Jamie and Elin's characters were portrayed sensitively. In order to support their work helping children in Scotland live in safe, loving families, building strong communities and protecting children's rights:

20% of the author royalties for this novel will be donated to Children 1st.

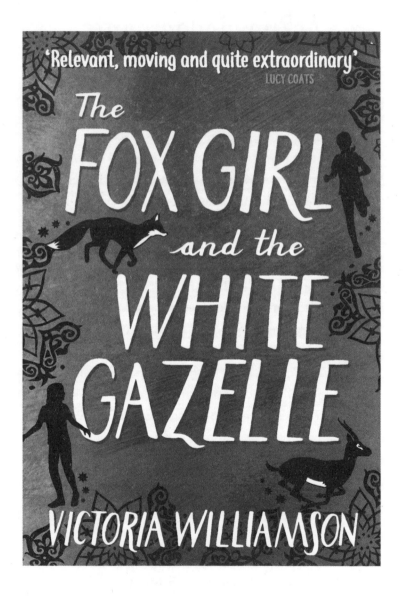

'Relevant, moving and quite extraordinary'
LUCY COATS

The
FOX GIRL
and the
WHITE
GAZELLE

VICTORIA WILLIAMSON

She is the Fox Girl.
I am the White Gazelle.
Together we can outrun anything.

Reema feels completely lost. She'll never call this strange
country, with its grey skies and boring food, home. Syria
is her home and it's a million miles away.

Caylin feels completely alone. She's looking after her
useless mum, stealing from other kids so she can eat. She
can't tell anyone, they'll only let her down.

The refugee and the bully – Reema and Caylin can't
imagine being friends, until a shared secret brings them
together.

Branford Boase Award Longlist
Read for Empathy Guide 2019
An USSBY Outstanding International Book

Turn over to read an extract!

CAYLIN

I sit up in bed with a start. A loud cry in the night shook me awake, and I hold my breath, listening. I don't think it came from Mum's room. I think it came from outside.

I scramble over to the window and peer out into the night. In the moonlight the Drumhill estate is silent, the quiet only disturbed every few minutes by the planes that roar overhead to Glasgow airport. I look down at the wee strip of ground behind our flats. The Council calls it a garden, but it's just a muddy dumping ground full of weeds and scrawny bushes that has a path leading up to the bin shed by the back wall.

I hear the cry again, and I peer into the dark alley that runs between the back wall and the gardens of the flats opposite. It's not coming from there though, the noise is closer than that.

It's coming from our bin shed.

I don't know what it is that makes me grab my jacket and go down to take a look.

Maybe there's a dog out there that's been hurt, or maybe it's a little kid who's gone missing like the one I saw on the news tonight, and I can be a hero by finding him first.

I hurry down the stairs, my slippers silent on the concrete steps.

It's all quiet for a minute, and then another plane passes so low on its way to the airport I'm half-scared it'll take our roof off.

When the engine roar finally fades away in the distance I hear something else.

Shuffling.

Snuffling.

A funny kind of whining.

It's coming from the bin shed, but when I go to look there's nothing there but smelly black bags. I check behind them. Nothing.

The noises have gone quiet, like something's heard me and is holding its breath.

That's when I think to look behind the shed.

I nearly jump out of my skin when I see yellow eyes staring back at me.

It's a fox, and she growls at me so fierce and low that I want to run straight back up to my room. I'm about to leave her be, when I see there's something wrong with her. She has a red coat and a dirty white belly with a big dark patch that's heaving up and down. It looks like she's struggling for breath, but when I take another step towards her I can see the dark patch is actually a huddle of tiny cubs all sucking hard for milk. The fox looks too skinny to be able to feed them.

I stare at them, a warm feeling of wonder filling up the dark places in my stomach that are usually big holes of worry and hunger and guilt. The fox is trying to get up and move away, but her front leg is bleeding and won't hold her weight. She looks like she's been hit by a car. The blind cubs are all shaken loose when she moves and start whimpering for milk. It makes me feel so sad I want to cry.

Feeling brave, I pull off my jacket and tuck it round them, trying to avoid the snapping jaws of the fox. She looks as hungry as I do at the end of the week when the benefits money runs out. I didn't buy anything at the shops today that I can give them, but tomorrow's Friday, when Mum'll have her money for the next week paid straight into her account. I know her number, so I'll nip down to the cash machine and get out enough to buy food for the foxes and pay the electricity bill.

If Mum wants to make a fuss about it she can drag herself out of bed for once and stop me.

Huh, like that's ever going to happen.

I'll have food for the foxes tomorrow. Tonight they'll have to make do with my old jacket. The fox is too tired to do more than snarl at me feebly, but when she sees I haven't taken her cubs, and feels the warmth from my jacket, she stops growling and just stares back at me with those big yellow eyes.

"I'm Caylin," I tell her, "and I'm going to look after you."

The warm feeling spreads when I say this until my whole body's tingling with happiness. "I'll keep you safe, you and your cubs. I'll keep you warm and fed, I'll keep you hidden. I'll keep you secret – I'm good at secrets."

This fox is my responsibility. A secret that doesn't make me sick to my stomach for once.

My best secret.

Mine.

REEMA

The loud cry in the night gives me such a fright I nearly drop my glass of water in the sink.

What was that?

I shiver in the dark kitchen, gritting my teeth until the roar of another passenger jet flying overhead dies away. I wait, but I do not hear the strange cry again.

I tiptoe back through the living room, silently cursing the people who put us in an apartment so close to an airport, when every memory we have is haunted by screaming aircraft engines and the fear of falling bombs.

Before I can reach my room though, a long howl wails through the corridor outside. I hurry up the narrow hall and press my ear to the front door, listening carefully. I think I hear footsteps dying away on the stairs.

I heard footsteps in the streets of Aleppo at night too. When the war began soldiers came banging on doors in the dark. I was so scared they would take Baba and Jamal away, there were some nights I would pray non-stop until the sun came up.

I should go back to bed…

Instead I take my coat from the rack on the wall and pull it over my nightdress. Then I open the door carefully, and peer into the dark corridor beyond.

I tiptoe out into the corridor, following the cold breeze to the back entrance that leads to a little wilderness beyond.

A soft growling whine is coming from the shelter full of trash cans at the bottom of the garden. I step onto the path and tiptoe closer.

I tilt my head and listen again, hearing snuffling and whining and soft, low whimpers. I pick up a heavy stick and peer into the space between the back of the shelter and the garden's stone wall. What I see there makes me drop the stick in surprise.

It is a family of foxes, all wrapped up in a smelly old coat. The mother blinks at me in the moonlight, wary and warning, but I can see she is injured and in no state to care for the cubs that are sucking desperately for milk.

She is hungry. They all are.

I turn and run back up the path, leaving the front door of our apartment wide open in my haste to get to the kitchen.

What do foxes eat? I wonder, rummaging around in the fridge. *I wish Jamal was here. He would know.*

I remember the time he rescued a bag full of puppies from the Queiq River. Baba would not have them in the house. But for months Jamal paid his lunch money to the man who ran the bicycle repair shop near our apartment, to let him keep them in the back room. Baba didn't tell Jamal off, because the Quran teaches that we must be kind to animals.

I do not think Baba would like me feeding foxes like pet dogs though.

I put leftover rice and meat into a bowl and fill another with milk and eggs, before carrying them carefully out to the back garden. The fox growls, but as soon as she smells the food she tries to sit up. Her leg will not support her though, so I place the bowls next to her, careful not to touch her. She sniffs at the contents suspiciously, looking up at me with wary yellow eyes.

I take a step back, showing her I mean no harm.

At once she eats ravenously, slurping the milk before attacking the meat and rice. It is clear she has not eaten in days.

"I am Reema," I tell the fox, "and I will not let you and your cubs go hungry."

The fox stops eating for a long moment and stares at me. I do not know if she understands, but the suspicion has gone from her eyes.

"You need a name," I say. But what she really needs is the freedom to run wild again and look after her young by herself. A name is all is have to offer her tonight.

"I will call you *Hurriyah*," I say softly in Arabic, and then in halting English I add, "I will... call you... *Freedom*."

I smile in the darkness as I gaze at Hurriyah and her cubs cuddled up in the old coat.

For the first time in this strange land I have something I can call my own, something to care about and hope for.

Something called Freedom.

The story continues in

The
FOX GIRL *and the* WHITE GAZELLE

About the Author

Victoria Williamson is a former primary school teacher from Scotland who has taught in schools around the world, including in Cameroon, Malawi and China. She has a Master's degree in special needs education, and has worked in the UK with children who have additional support needs. Her critically acclaimed debut novel, *The Fox Girl and the White Gazelle* was inspired by Victoria's experience teaching in a school where many pupils were seeking asylum.

Victoria divides her time between writing, visiting schools and libraries, and speaking at literary festivals. Her stories feature the voices of some of the many children she's met over the years on her real-life adventures around the world.

Find Victoria on Twitter @strangelymagic.